CROSSING LINES

PAMELA ELLEN FERGUSON

Border Coombe Press

CROSSING LINES

CROSSING LINES is a work of fiction though many of the themes will be all too familiar to those involved in the multilayered politics and hardships of the Border. The characters are fictional and are not based on any specific person, living or deceased. The author has made every effort to ensure this. Any overlaps are purely coincidental.

Special appreciation for ***TEXAS MONTHLY*** and Dr Cecilia Balli, Anthropologist and Journalist, for permission to quote a passage verbatim in Chapter 11 from Dr Balli's article on the Juarez femicides titled *Ciudad de la Muerte* published in ***TM's*** June 2003 issue.

ISBN: 978-0-9966679-0-6 (paperback)
ISBN: 978-0-9966679-1-3 (eBook)

Published
by
Border Coombe Press
Austin, Texas

www.pamelaferguson.net

Additional Books by Pamela Ellen Ferguson

The Palestine Problem	1973
The Pipedream	1974
The Olympic Mission	1976
Dominion	1977
The Sacrifice	1981
Decoration and Design for the '80s	1983
The Self-Shiatsu Handbook	1995
Take Five	2000
Sand to Sky (co-edited with Debra Duncan Persinger, PhD)	2008
Sunshine Picklelime	2010

Dedicated to the activists at
Austin Tan Cerca de la Frontera
for their tireless support of
maquiladora workers and families.

and

In loving memory of the victims
of femicide in the killing fields of
Juarez, Chihuahua Mexico,
the state where I was born.

CHAPTER 1
Friday

I'll describe events of that week to you exactly as they happened otherwise you won't believe me. A murder to solve during Halloween? Oh come on ! I'm a 38 year old architect not a sleuth. But during those days I had to be everything, including a surrogate parent. Nothing prepared me for this experience. You remember my Irish mother and how she used to remind us about the spirit of Samhein—the Celtic origin of Halloween —when ghosts of the departed visit loved ones? She would place extra teacups on the table for my late father and grandparents. Except this year I included a cup for her and my brother Hugh. I evoked her spirit for strength as often as I cursed Hugh's for leaving me his mess. So here goes. Friday night. One Halloween. Buckle up.

Winds blasted through Austin with venom. Sleep was impossible, so I went up to my deck with my cats Doris and Horis in the small hours armed with a basket of trick-or-treat leftovers. My cathedral chimes clanged with such vigor, a neighbor texted to complain.

Something tumbled out of one of the pecan trees swaying opposite my deck. Sensor lights popped on. I would have ignored it but Doris and Horis began growling and pacing.

Branch?

Raccoon?

Large squirrel nest?

My curiosity piqued. Lady Bird Lake looked black below the hike-and-bike trail that cut across the lower edge of my property. Grabbing flashlight and cell phone I skipped downstairs as the cats bounded ahead of me to take a look.

The object turned out to be a Halloween head with a slashed face. It dangled off my polka dot lantana bush, straw-like hair matted with fake blood. Another prank by local kids? Ghouls, skeletons and ghosts had been swinging dizzily off trees all week. I reached out and grabbed the head to pry it loose.

Jesus Christ! It was cold.

I dialed emergency.

"Austin 911. Do you need Police, Fire, or EMS?"

"Police. A human head fell out of my pecan tree—"

"Ma'am." Deep sigh. "It's Halloween—"

"Hey, no kidding? Great time to behead someone with shaggy hair and dump it near my home."

"Ma'am, this is the fifteenth prank call—"

"Why don't I text you a pic?"

"No need for that, ma'am. Exact location?"

I told him how cops could find me above the hike-and-bike trail.

Then I hunkered down and beamed my flashlight around the head. The slashed face and jagged scar on his neck couldn't distort softly youthful features. Dark roots were just visible under his thatch. A young Latino teenager perhaps? A white mask lay close by. Dropped by the perp? The cats sniffed around, hissed, and retreated.

I rose and looked away, needing a moment of tranquility to restore dignity to the youth. I swept my flashlight in an arc but could not see any other body parts. Where had I seen his face before? Downtown bus stops? Hawking drugs on the Drag opposite campus?

Or was he one of those kids hanging around day laborers on the corner of a weedy lot a block away, baggy pants dragging in the dust? I looked at him again and snapped shots with my cell phone, hoping to jog my memory. A runaway? Beheaded over a human smuggling deal gone sour? Chain-saw beheadings happened on the other side of the Border, victims of drug cartels. But a beheading in *Austin?* Or was this a random attack by local vigilantes to send a message to youth desperate to flee violence in El Salvador or Nicaragua? And why place the head in *my* tree?

Sirens wailed close by.

Within minutes, vehicles pulled up in the road.

Flashlights splintered the darkness.

"Down here!" I shouted.

"Ms. McBride?"

A couple of uniformed cops appeared through the trees. Everything moved quickly. The cats darted away. Lights splayed around my orange sweatpants and hoodie. Until cops decided I wasn't some wacko. One officer set up powerful spotlights and barked details into the walkie-talkie attached to his shoulder. Another began to unravel yellow crime-scene tape to secure the site. He fired questions at me. How did I discover the head? Where exactly did I live? Did I notice anyone on the path?

"The head dropped off that branch," I said, pointing He followed the trajectory and glanced from left to right.

More vehicles began pulling up in the road.

Within minutes a voice said, "Detective Zuniga. Homicide."

Zuniga looked more like a model arriving for a front cover fashion shoot. Bubbly black hair. Dimpled face. A weight lifter's torso and trim hips. Designer chinos and a crisply ironed shirt the color of bing cherries.

Masked and gloved crime-scene technicians followed behind and fanned out like moths around the bushes.

I heard myself say, "It's just a kid." Zuniga glanced down at the head, then, eyeing my pumpkin colored crocs, he said, "You stood next to the victim, right?" He nodded at one of the crime-scene techs to photograph my crocs, including the soles.

"I also touched the kid's head. Hey, I thought it was a Halloween prank. You want to scan my fingerprints too?" I asked as I raised one foot after the other for the camera.

"Later if necessary. We need you to leave the crime scene. Now. I'll take your statement in a while," Zuniga said, pointing toward the path.

Reluctantly, I padded back toward my deck to watch the action below. As if on cue, the wind had settled down.

I overheard bantering.

"I lefffffft my hearrrrrrrrt in San Fran-cis-cooooo ... and found my head at Lady Bird Lake ... o," crooned a tech as he crouched down to make casts of shoe impressions.

I couldn't blame him for adding humor to a grisly task.

An investigator I recognized from the medical examiner's unit appeared, buttoning a jacket over her layered green party costume like the character Poison Ivy from *Batman.*

Photographs were snapped from all angles. Objects were plucked and bagged off the surrounding bushes and pathway.

Brutal death. Brisk cleanup.

I closed my eyes. A long freight train clattered across the rusted old railway bridge over the lake. Downtown Austin was waking up.

If I listened carefully, I could hear the walls of my converted railyard home responding. Calls of generations of rail men, echoes of a busy past, of goods and produce docked below in the days when ferries served this part of the Colorado River, now known as Lady Bird Lake, which separated downtown from South Austin. The sounds were reassuring, a contrast to a crime scene flooded by lights.

I watched the medical investigator pull on a pair of purple gloves, lean over the head and untangle an object out of the thatch of hair. She flipped it open, straightened, then showed the object to Detective Zuniga. Both glanced up at me.

She zipped the object into an evidence bag and handed it to the detective.

"Ms. McBride?" He called out.

"Detective?"

"The night's always darkest before the dawn," he said, walking up the path toward me. "My mother's favorite Spanish proverb. It helps at such times."

"It does?" I asked.

"Can we talk inside? I'd like you to examine this," he said, holding up the bag.

Babyish looks. But he was as alert as a panther. But older than I originally assumed. I went down to let him in.

Late thirties perhaps? Roughly my own age? His eyes swept my living space.

"You're an *architect?*" he said.

He asked in a way that made me think he expected architects to live in high-tech spaces. Not in a converted rail-yard structure above Lady Bird Lake with an interior shaped out of recycled materials dominated by a curvy mesquite bar I'd salvaged out of an old West Texas brothel. He glanced out of the window, eyeing the snakes-and-ladder arrangement I built for the cats to access the deck.

Below us, crime scene specialists fluttered around the cacti, cypress, live oak and pecan trees that bordered my property and the hike-and-bike trail.

Then Zuniga perched on a bar stool. "You recognize the victim?" He asked.

I shook my head. "*Might* have been a kid I saw hanging around day laborers near Fifth Street," I said.

He pulled on a pair of gloves from his pocket. Using thumb and forefinger, he reached into the bag to part the pages of a dark blue American passport.

I stared, stunned. My nephew Rory's photo grinned at me, a goofy shot taken his freshman year, tawny hair looking like Cowardly Lion in *The Wizard of Oz*. In a flash, I saw the thatch of the butchered kid. With that hair, any fool could pass as Rory.

"I don't understand," I frowned. "The vic isn't my nephew."

"Violent death can distort features."

"C'mon, detective! The victim looks like a teenager. My nephew's twenty-one."

"Go take a closer look."

"Detective, I don't need to. I'd recognize my nephew anywhere." I reached for my phone and speed-dialed Rory's number. Voicemail. Damn.

I texted him and then remembered he was on a field trip. Which meant he could be anywhere. Or out of range, I told Zuniga. Of all the moments.

"Your nephew mention anything recently about being mugged?" Zuniga zipped the evidence bag and removed his gloves. "I'll check if he reported a stolen or lost passport," he said, tapping keys on a cell phone.

"Rory probably dropped it somewhere near campus and doesn't even *know* it's missing." I shrugged. "He's an airhead."

"Mind if I record our conversation?"

"Why? I gave details to the first officer."

"A formality," he explained, placing his cell phone between us on the bar. "Ms. McBride, you claim you discovered the head and called 911 around 4:37. What, you just happened to be up at that time? About to go jogging?"

I found his calm tone and body language unsettling.

"Am I a suspect?"

Zuniga gave a dimpled smile. "I'm figuring out time lines."

"I can't sleep when it's this windy," I said. "I was on my deck munching leftover trick-or-treat stash."

"You didn't hear anyone?"

"Over the sound of those cathedral chimes? No way!"

He wasn't convinced. "Your famous brother Hugh McBride was Rory's father, right?"

"Sure. What does that have to do with anything?" I asked.

"The media'll be staked out here soon."

"Oh man. That's all I need."

Hugh, my late brother, created network TV's investigative *McBride Reports* with a knack for global hot spots, disaster zones, and sleazy business deals involving drug cartels and corrupt officials. Hugh's reports didn't endear him to certain moguls of industry, or the politicians they pampered. Rory was a journalism major at U.T. But I hoped he wouldn't follow his father's footsteps.

"Your brother made a lot of enemies," Zuniga said. "Someone may be settling old scores and mistook the victim for your nephew."

"No way." I tried to sound dismissive, but my stomach flipped.

I wanted to believe this was too far-fetched to be plausible.

Zuniga tapped his cell phone and gazed up at my pressed-tin ceiling. "How come you swung residential rights in a commercial zone? Who owed your brother a favor at City Hall?"

"No one," I said. "I sleep with the mayor and entire planning committee."

"So that's how it's done." He chuckled.

It broke the ice.

Playing the naive card, I launched into an explanation of changes in zoning laws during the economic downside to boost this scruffy stretch between the lake and Fifth Street, close to the Amtrak station. I bought and converted a line of single-story flat-roofed structures into colorful multi-use studios that were snapped up by designers, photographers and start-ups.

My rail-yard home and nearby studio transformed a crumbling limestone building and lofty depot that once served freight railway lines for goods shipped along the Colorado River.

We all formed a funky pocket community under a skyline now spiked by skinny skyscrapers between us and Fifth Street. I stepped from our world into theirs when I walked by their fitness studios, hair salons and pampered pet clinics.

Zuniga checked my windows to scope the mixed surroundings and, I assumed, to figure out how much I could see at night.

A noise outside my front window caught our attention. One of the crime-scene techs was busily scaling the tree above the head. Straddling the branches, he took photographs, and tweezered off items snagged in the bark.

Zuniga's phone hummed. He lifted it to his ear and glanced at me. He assumed I didn't understand when he instructed someone in Spanish to check my nephew's apartment.

"I told you my nephew isn't in town," I said, when the call ended.

"Rory hasn't filed a lost or stolen passport report," he replied, without missing a beat. "It was used recently at the Border. We'll check the time against surveillance cameras to see who crossed the bridge. Your nephew or the decedent,"

"The *Border?* Where?"

"I can't share those details."

"Detective, if Rory's in trouble I'd be the first to know," I said.

Zuniga handed me his card. "Call me soon as you hear from him. Day or night."

I walked Zuniga out of the door and watched as he handed the evidence bag to one of the crime scene techs. I sensed he had sidestepped protocol to show me the passport. Sensitivity? Or to check my reaction?

The victim's head was zipped into a baby-sized blue bag and carried with the rest of the evidence to vehicles parked along the street. Spotlights were switched off and dismantled. Only the yellow tape remained. The cats belted inside as the vehicles pulled away.

Dawn began to inch across the sky.

The card gave his full name. *Eduardo Zuniga.*

Hmmm. His Spanish sounded like an unusual mix of Tex-Mex and other influences I couldn't quite catch. I made a mistake assuming he was just a pretty face.

I checked my phone. Not a peep out of Rory. Now I began to feel queasy. I knew I had to go through his apartment before that wily detective came up with a search warrant.

CHAPTER 2
Saturday

As Zuniga predicted, TV vans from local affiliates of national news channels began pulling up outside at daybreak. A couple of uniformed cops kept them off my property and directed early-morning joggers and dog walkers to the hike-and-bike trail beyond the yellow tape.

A patrol car was parked close by. The *Jumping Bean* coffee shop just across from me was doing a roaring trade. Reporters, gawkers and cyclists lined the enclosed porch and steps of the cute 1930s compact tan-and-chocolate-trimmed wooden house.

I could kiss privacy good-bye. I put on a gray hooded sweat suit, slung my wireless headset around my neck, ignored my yellow jeep and made a quick exit on my bike out of a side door around the back of a nearby photography studio and past one of the skyscrapers onto the street. Beyond the sight lines of the TV cameras, I then zigzagged through traffic to the heart of downtown Austin, toward the Capitol and shortcuts to campus.

Rory still hadn't returned my calls or text messages. I began to feel desperate. Rory was more like a son than a nephew. I helped Hugh raise him after my sister-in-law, Penny, just quit one day and returned home to Canada. My mother and I traded off ferrying Rory to school or collecting him in the middle of the night if Hugh was suddenly called on assignment. We took him to games and dental appointments and shopping for clothes. One time I dropped tools and flew to San Francisco to rescue him when Hugh was held up miles away after leaving 10 year old Rory alone in a hotel room. All of which was tough on the boy but he refused to show it. "The guys say it's super cool to have such a famous Dad," he'd insist. Rory dealt with grief by being aloof and hostile since his father's death, insisting he needed "space."

Space? Losing his passport?

The simplest explanation was this. His passport tumbled out of a backpack on campus when he was distracted. Some street kid picked it up, frizzed out his hair to look like my nephew and got himself killed hustling drugs or sex or whatever.

No. Too easy.

OK, complex. Rory was researching a story on street kids or undocumented workers and offered the boy his passport to keep cops off his back.

No, that didn't cut it either.

At some point, navigating my way through a busy corner near campus, I thought I heard someone call my name, Elspeth, but ignored it. Those closest to me always used my nickname, Buzzy.

Rory lived in a typical student's apartment in a two-story vanilla-brick complex a block from campus, just off the Drag, as that bustling twenty-four-hour slice of Guadalupe Street was called. It provided all the contrasts of student life: funky vintage clothing, noodle bowls, bank-o-mats, donuts and coffee, a University co-op and a gaudy tattoo shop. Assorted drugged-out sidewalk dwellers wandered up and down looking for fast deals and sugar hits.

Rory's beat up old orange VW Beetle wasn't parked outside. Pizza and Thai food delivery fliers hung off his front doorknob, as usual. I stepped over candy wrappers from trick-or-treaters and let myself in with my spare set of keys.

The place looked even more chaotic than usual. There was a hint of sage and cedar in the air, which told me someone else was here recently, and Rory was not. He was acutely allergic to incense.

Friends and out of towners used his place like a hostel.

Hard to know who owned or dumped what.

Mounds of papers and files sloped from the side of the computer down to the rug. Books were crammed along shelves covering three walls from floor to ceiling. Rumpled sheets and pillows covered his futon.

The TV was on but there was no sound. The image rolled and jumped. I realized it was on DVD mode so pressed the eject button. There was no label. I fiddled with the remote control and pressed Play. It slid back into the slot. OK, just a home video. It looked like a bunch of young guys swigging beers and sharing hits of pot in an open desert setting under the stars. Headlights from someone's car illuminated the scene. The camera swayed left and right and swung upside down like a dancer. Hazy shapes fought in the background. One shape was dragged out of view. I caught a brief glimpse of open scrubland. West Texas? Chihuahua Desert?

Everything changed in a flash.

Two burly guys dragged a slim, naked young woman by her legs into the center of the group. I couldn't see her face. She struggled so violently that two extra guys held her down and kicked her legs apart. There was no sound, but that made her silent screams even more horrifying.

Blood spurted on the lens. I hit stop, quickly ejected and pocketed the DVD, intending to confront my nephew with it. I couldn't *believe* he watched such brutality. Those guys weren't actors. Disgusted, I went into the bathroom, fearing I might throw up, and splashed cold water on my face. The towels were filthy, covered with black stains. I dried my face with toilet paper. Rory wasn't the neatest guy but he wasn't a slob like this. Clumps of tawny hair clogged the sink. Rory's hair?

But who was using black dye in his bathroom, and why?

Puzzled, I returned to the main room. Dirty dishes cluttered the sink. Stained pizza boxes stuck out of the garbage can. I resisted a temptation to clean up. Instead I used a red marker to scribble a message for Rory—or anyone else—to call me immediately. I stuck it on the fridge door with a Snoopy magnet and checked my cell phone again. Still no word from Rory. I sent yet more "life/death" voicemails and texts. I also reached for his landline and called him from there—just in case he was avoiding my caller ID and thought the call was from someone using his place. Still no answer.

As I turned around, I kicked something soft. It was one of my brother's sweaty old gym bags, bulging with cast-off clothes. I picked up a tattered McBride tartan shirt Hugh inherited from our father, a few belts, a Longhorns T-shirt he used for the gym, a hooded fleece sweatshirt and a couple of sweatpants. Odd. I replaced them in the bag, wondering why Rory held on to clothes we had sorted and he promised to drop off at *Goodwill.*

I could understand my nephew wanting Hugh's worn suede or designer leather jackets, sweaters and Mandela shirts. But sweaty gym clothes?

A file folder of Hugh's photos lay beside the bed. Marriage photos, shots of Hugh holding young Rory, teenage shots of Hugh and me with our parents. A pic of Hugh in his signature khaki years before the *Gap* made it fashionable.

There was also a shot of Hugh in front of a TV camera on a tough assignment no one else wanted in Yemen, and an early shot of him stepping between victims of cartel violence in Juarez.

I continued idling through the mess on Rory's desk and picked up a pink binder. It held recent printouts of land development projects in the Rio de la Luna area of West Texas, one of the rivers that fed the Rio Grande. The simple logo of a few vertical lines crossed by short horizontal lines caught my eye. It looked vaguely familiar but I couldn't remember why. Rory hadn't mentioned anything or tapped my resources as usual over any topic related to land development, for some college assignment. I tossed it onto the mess, something I was to regret in the days ahead.

I examined his landline once again to check outgoing and incoming calls. Four calls came from *Isabel's Tamales.* Two calls were to a Ruben Flores at the same area code. I checked the code—it was the Border town of Del Rio, where Rory was born. I felt chilled, wondering if he was on some personal quest he selected not to tell me. I added the numbers to the contact list on my cell phone.

I then eased a Visa bill out of the clutter, dialed the 1-800 number, punched in the account number and "O" to talk to customer service.

Lowering my voice to Rory's husky tones, I said, "Hey, this is Rory McBride. I can't remember the last time I used my card!"

"No problem, Mr. McBride. For security reasons, could I have your mother's maiden name?"

"Sure. Cameron."

"Thank you, Mr. McBride. Your last charge was four days ago. *Garcia Gas.*"

"*Yes!* You have the phone number?"

She quoted a number with the same area code. Del Rio.

I thanked her. She told me to "have myself a wonderful day" and said goodbye.

Still no word from Rory.

I continued to hunt around, remembering what Detective Zuniga said about Rory's passport being used recently at the Border. He refused to tell me where, but now I knew it was probably the Del Rio bridge. If Rory had been mugged or injured at the Border, wouldn't I be the first to know?

My mind was so full of what ifs that I tripped over a scruffy pair of sneakers near the front door. They had an unusual zigzag logo, and were too narrow to be Rory's.

All I could do was hope the owner of the sneakers returned, noticed my note on the fridge and called me. There was no way I could sit around and wait for that to happen. I had to keep moving.

As this was Saturday, I planned to leave immediately for the Border.

CHAPTER 3

By the time I cycled home, I could hardly see the *Jumping Bean* coffee shop for people. Saturday's usual brunch crowd had quadrupled because of the news. Lazy strains of alto sax wafted through open windows.

It had turned into a balmy fall day without the edgy winds of last night. Trees surrounding my rail-yard showed all the intense shades of pink, crimson and bright yellow, more so than in previous years. What a backdrop for a grisly crime.

A local TV cameraman spotted me trying to sneak in and came running toward me, followed by the others. I pushed back my hoodie and said, "Guys, Detective Zuniga's handling the case. No comments at this time, OK?"

Ignoring the babel of questions like *"Is the beheading linked to one of your brother's past investigations of the Mexican drug cartels?"* or *"do you fear for your own life, Ms. McBride?"* I turned and wheeled my bike inside. My cell phone chirped. Zuniga. He wanted updates on Rory. I didn't have any.

"You tried his friends?"

I said that was next on my list.

"Girlfriends?"

"I'll call you when I hear from him," I said, reluctant to get into any personal details about my nephew's life. In fact Rory admitted he hadn't dated anyone seriously since Hugh's death. Just a couple of hook-ups.

The last girlfriend he had was months ago. She ditched him for some "jerk of a jock," my nephew told me in disgust.

I asked Zuniga if he had an image off the surveillance cameras at the Border, but didn't say I suspected it was the Del Rio/Acuña crossing.

"We're still examining footage," he said.

"Anything in your database match the victim's ID?"

"Nada," he said. "We're running an artist's sketch on TV's *Crime Tips* later." He paused before adding, "There's no match to any missing person profile."

"You'd tell me if . . . other parts of the body turn up?"

"Nothing in the vicinity of your home, if that's what's worrying you. Victim was killed elsewhere. M.E. says the head was transported in a cooler. Which means someone deliberately placed that head facing your deck."

I didn't respond.

"Meaning," he went on, "this *could* be a revenge killing."

I couldn't think of any reason why someone would want to savage Rory or hurt me because of something my late brother exposed or reported. I told him again that my brother received so many threats it would be impossible to single one out. I dreaded being in the center of a high-profile case. I wanted the police to focus on the victim and not on the McBrides. Was the victim just some throwaway kid smuggled across the Border with others? Did he have a desperate family somewhere? Mexico? Nicaragua? El Salvador?

I just remembered that white mask lying beside the head and asked Zuniga if it was linked to the victim? Or something trick-or-treaters dropped?

"Crime lab's checking it for trace evidence."

Two possibilities occurred to me. Either the mask had been placed over the victim's face by someone in a mock parody of Halloween or *El Día de los Muertos,* or the killer knew the victim and tried to shield his brutalized face. I shared my thoughts with Zuniga.

"We're not ruling anything out," he said. Then, "Ms. McBride?"

"Detective?"

"You visited your nephew's apartment this morning?"

"You had me *followed?*"

"One of our patrol cars reported seeing you there."

"You're staking out his apartment?"

"If your nephew was the intended target, it won't take long for someone to figure out they beheaded the wrong guy."

"Detective, I'll kill him before they find him."

"Your brother ever use your nephew as an intern? A researcher?"

"Sure, assignments here and there."

I didn't know details but I knew Zuniga was fishing, so I ended the call. I hid the DVD that I'd lifted from Rory's apartment in a secret spot under my bar counter, then picked up my tablet, and zipped it with some overnight gear into a gym bag. I hoped the media would assume I planned to work out when I walked by in a few minutes.

I left a message for my architectural design assistant, Carlos dos Santos, to feed Doris and Horis who followed him around adoringly, and open our studio on Monday morning in case I returned late. Fortunately we had no meetings scheduled with clients or site visits until Wednesday.

I couldn't even think about design projects or the next class I had to teach at U.T. I spent a few moments centering myself to avoid conveying any anxiety when I ran the media gauntlet outside.

It worked. The crowd was actually beginning to dwindle around the *Jumping Bean.* I knew more media would return in time for the evening news. By then I'd be at the Border. I left my yellow jeep in the parking lot and crossed to a path behind the neighboring photography studio toward the gym close by on Fifth Street. Making sure I wasn't being followed, I quickly jogged to a nearby car rental, selected a new sports model with tinted windows, and programmed my Bluetooth.

Within thirty minutes I was on the road, heading west toward the Border town of Del Rio. This also gave me thinking time. I explored all options, realizing I had no way of knowing if the Del Rio calls on Rory's phone were for him or whoever was staying in his apartment.

Rory was born in Del Rio, where Hugh had done some of his rookie reporting and had met a group of Canadian students backpacking along the Rio Grande. The group included a wild young nineteen-year-old named Penny Cameron, who left the group and moved in with Hugh the day they met in a bar.

They married some months later, when Penny discovered she was pregnant with Rory.

I always liked Penny's bouncy resilience and knew she also jumped into the marriage to escape a controlling pastor of a father.

I never really understood why she suddenly upped and left Del Rio and returned to British Columbia when Rory was a little boy, resulting in a bitter custody battle. My efforts to reach out to her failed. Hugh refused to talk about it.

So I wasn't way out of line wondering if the Del Rio calls on Rory's landline reflected an inner quest on his part to complete something from his own—or his parents'—past. The name *Isabel's Tamales* kept pinging in my memory from that time but I couldn't pinpoint a link.

Our family lawyer Grace Colvin called about an hour outside Austin. I was heading toward Fredericksburg, deep in the Hill Country, driving by shuttered farm stalls with names like Vogel and Engel, descendants of the original German families who settled this fertile stretch of golden peach orchard country.

"Buzzy, you're all over the news. What the hell's going on?"

I quickly brought her up to speed, realizing I should have contacted her earlier.

"Zuniga's on the case?" said Grace, her voice rising an octave. "He's like a pit bull snapping at every detail. Woohoo. Known as Eddie 24/7 in the APD."

I said I underestimated him because of his baby face.

She hooted. "You and everyone else. He plays the dimpled card brilliantly. Folks let their guard down around him."

"Well I won't." I told her about Rory's passport and my suspicions about a possible stolen identity involving some poor kid with dyed frizzy hair. Admitting I was desperate to find my nephew, I said, "Zuniga believes Rory was the intended target."

"Hugh McBride's son? And you didn't call me? You know what the media will make of this? Haul your nephew's ass into my office. Uh huh, it's Saturday and I'm working."

"Grace, OK, I get the point. I'm headed west to the Border." I told her Rory wasn't responding to any of my calls. I suspected he was in the Del Rio area, possibly out of range.

"Say *what?* Can I believe I'm hearing this? Not another word to Zuniga—or the media—unless I'm with you. Once you find Master-I-need-space Rory, call me. Buzzy, you're way out of your league. Austin's greenest architect cycling around town trying to figure why someone's beheaded on her property? Give me a *break!*"

I pulled over to the side of the road under a sign for one of the new wineries. Grace's intensity was too dangerous to handle on speakerphone while driving. She was more than our lawyer, having become a close family friend years ago after she represented Hugh in a libel case. I could visualize her pacing her office, a tall willowy African American, gray hair sculpted close to her head, spiral earrings bouncing, a long silk scarf reaching almost to the tips of her hand-tooled boots. She grew up in a one-eyed East Texas town and paid her way through law school serving in a live blues bar in the hub of Austin's Sixth Street music scene.

Grace knew how to work the system, with an attitude sharpened by being black, female and brilliant in a State that had lynched her grandfather.

I shared my unease about Rory's safety, especially after snooping around his apartment. I didn't say anything about finding that grotesque DVD.

Grace listened without butting in.

"Check in with me every couple of hours, hear what I'm saying? I'll see what I can squeeze out of Zuniga. Does he know you're on the road?"

"No."

"Good. Don't spike his curiosity. Buzz, take care of yourself. Touch base ASAP." Grace suddenly sounded very quiet and serious.

"I will, Grace. And thanks."

After we ended the call, I sat there staring across the empty peach tree orchards and vineyards, wondering if I should just turn around and go home instead of racing to the Border because of a gut feeling. I hit the button for the classical music station and kept going.

It took me over three hours to wind my way out of the gently rolling Hill Country. My route then cut through craggy limestone cliffs. Soon everything flattened into scrubby West Texas landscape leading toward the Border. Views of juniper, live oak and cypress gave way to mesquite, prickly pear, sagebrush and tumbleweed. Herds of grazing sheep dotted my view here and there.

Avoiding the anonymity of the major highways, I needed a beautiful drive to balance the horror of the night.

Above, puffs of cloud chased one another across the canopy of an expansive sky. An occasional windmill spiked the horizon. I switched channels to check the weather report.

Chunks of the area had recently experienced flash flooding but there was little evidence of that here. Drought-blackened cacti punctuated my route. Closer to *la frontera,* assorted Spanish-language and music stations dominated the local airwaves.

I recognized the late popular Tejana star Selena singing, *No me queda mas. … Que perderme en un abismo … de Tristeza … y lagrimas. . . .*

As her lovely voice filled the interior of my rental car, I recalled clips of Hugh's report on her modest Corpus Christi *barrio* and nearby recording studio. After her assassination, the network ran several clips from his reports. When Selena finished her song, I pulled into the parking lot of a convenience store, just after the *Welcome/Bienvenidos* sign for Del Rio, the Val Verde county seat, population 35,000 and a sprawling version of the town I remembered. I was also quick to notice the warning *Be Careful Where You Drill* signs.

I checked GPS to locate *Garcia Gas.* It was only a couple of miles ahead on the industrial outskirts.

I needed to tank up anyway. This would be a good place to start making a few inquiries, I thought, as I pulled into a broken-down-looking business I could easily have missed had I not pinpointed its exact location. A car was jacked up in an open garage.

A glass door was half open, displaying a tiny office. Roadside welding equipment stood idle between the garage and a vine-smothered prefab.

Tejano music played at full blast.

An elderly Latino with a wrinkled face, overalls and a crumpled straw cowboy hat appeared at the office door, wiping his hands. "Buenas tardes, señora," he said politely.

"Buenas tardes. Llene el tanque, por favor?" I responded and then asked if he knew *Isabel's Tamales?*

"Que?"

"Isabel's Tamales, señor?"

"No, no good." He shook his head dismissively and said, "You want the best tamales? *Cocina Rosita.* Two blocks down." He nodded to the left.

I smiled and told him I had a business meeting at Isabel's.

"Ayyyeee," he said, rolling his eyes. "Not here. In Comstock." He swept his arm to the right. "Highway 90 west. Go, go, go, go. Until Comstock. After Amistad Lake."

When the pump clicked, he slowly removed the nozzle from my gas tank and replaced the cap. I reached through the car window for my purse, paid him, and then pulled out a photograph of Rory and asked if he recognized him.

He eyed me, glanced around, stared at my rental car and asked, *"Para que lo busca?"*

Sensing his wariness, I said innocently, "He's my nephew. I want to surprise him if he's still in town."

The man shook his head in disbelief. "Crazy hair?"

"That's him. You remember his car?"

Anyone would remember Rory's beat-up orange VW bug.

He shrugged and stared at me.

"It's OK," I said. *"No problema."*

He turned and disappeared into his office. I glanced in my rearview mirror, sensing his discomfort when I caught a glimpse of him watching me through his glass door. I hoped he didn't think I was a federal agent, snooping around to check his status. At least he confirmed Rory had been here recently.

I decided to keep going to Comstock, anxious to get most of my driving done before tiredness kicked in.

CHAPTER 4

Comstock was a small town about twenty-five miles northwest of Del Rio on the long stretch of Highway 90 west linking Amistad Dam and the nearby Seminole Canyon. The dam was not only a fisherman's paradise, but one of those joint Mexican-American ventures aimed to solve the Border's twin nightmares: crippling drought and flash floods. Limestone caves like the Fate Bell Shelter in Seminole Canyon had some of Texas's most famous ancient rock paintings, or pictographs, dating back over four thousand years. Very few Texans even *knew* about such archaeological gems.

All of this came back to me as I zoomed along, because I remembered visiting Hugh, Penny and little Rory during my student days, when Hugh worked this area. We had gone together to see the pictographs and argued about their meaning. I saw the red-and-black, mainly linear images of animals and people, possibly hunting scenes, as an ancient storyboard to teach children about history, myths and symbols. Penny thought the scenes invoked the power of shamans for protection or insight. I could still hear her adding, *"Look at the long vertical body of the shaman like figure with short arms spread out. Sort of mystical transformation. . . ."* Then I remembered her saying her Dad was a fundamentalist pastor who would probably shout her down or spin some theory about the figure predicting the crucifixion.

Hugh just laughed at both of us and said all he saw was "graffiti art" about killing animals. The overhanging cave and our discussions scrolled by in my memory. The view was West Texas in microcosm.

The huge, protected cave jutted out midway between the desertscape above and the densely vegetated slope, leading down to a craggy drop to the lower Pecos River, below.

For some reason my overwired architect's brain extracted that image of the long vertical lines crossed by short horizontal lines with the logo I'd spotted on the pink binder on Rory's desk that contained printouts on some Rio de la Luna land development proposals just east of where I was right now.

Anxiety threw me into a time warp. The acres of flat scrubland ahead of me on the road had changed little in a couple of decades. I kept imagining a youthful Hugh here, deeply tanned to a point where he blended with the people of the Border, more Latino than Anglo. We both inherited the Black Irish looks of our mother, thick black hair that turned gray prematurely, and olive skin.

Hugh, Penny and Rory had actually lived in one of Del Rio's *barrios* close to the Rio Grande, so Hugh could hop back and forth across the bridge to Acuña on the Mexican side.

I tried to clear past thoughts. Ahead, cacti and sagebrush dominated my view as far as the eye could see. The soil was the color of pale limestone, dashed here and there by outcrops of terra-cotta.

A motel sign announced *Lake View Rooms. Kitchenettes. Cable TV. Free Wi-Fi. Perfect for Fishermen.* The place was a rectangular arrangement of single-story brick buildings on the left. Followed by a bait and tackle shop and an RV site. Clusters of prefab houses, trailers and mobile homes stretched far back.

Patches of veggies and corn had been hacked out of the drought-ridden terrain. Washing flapped on a line between two metal posts. I drove on until I spotted a line of stores and a gas station.

An adjoining flat-topped adobe's sign said *Isabel's Tamales—Especialidades de la Casa.* I could tell it attracted a mixed crowd just from the cars in the parking lot. A white Border Patrol van with a green logo stood between a Lexus and a rusted fisherman's truck.

Two Border Patrol officers in dark green uniforms and sunglasses came out of Isabel's carrying doggy bags and climbed into their van. When they reversed, I swung into their space.

A striking woman with thick, wavy shoulder-length black hair was in the doorway saying good-bye to a group of businessmen.

From the easy bantering I guessed she was something of a local celebrity. Customers probably drove here from miles around.

I walked toward her. "Isabel?"

"Sure, I'm Isabel." She stared at me and smiled. "Hugh's little sister, right?"

Puzzled, I asked, "Have we met?"

"You came to one of my mother's *tamaladas* feasts? One December years ago with Hugh?"

Laughing at my expression, she said, "I was just a teenager then, why would you remember me? I was also at Hugh's funeral. Come in, Buzz."

I felt welcomed *and* embarrassed as I entered her bustling cafe.

The bar was festooned with *El Día de los Muertos* decorations, paper flowers and posters of Frida Kahlo. Wait staff moved between the Formica-topped tables carrying platters of assorted tamales. Just the smell reminded me how hungry I was.

Isabel took my order for a vegetarian variety, glanced over her shoulder and repeated it in Spanish to the cooks in an open kitchen.

"Good you came during my quiet time, Buzzy."

"You call this quiet?"

"Come back when it's busy." She smiled. As she turned away I dug into my memory, trying to place her. I remembered the *tamaladas* festival at her mother's home in Del Rio: long trestle tables arranged outside and folks arriving in relays for the annual celebration where guests fixed their own tamales. Kids and teenagers everywhere.

That seemed like a whole other world away compared with this stunning woman in an apple green polo shirt and designer jeans. Isabel gave the impression of being very much the successful Border businesswoman who moved fluently between both cultures. I wondered what her connection was with Hugh. She returned to my table with a delicious plate load of tamales and said casually, "You've come to see Rory? He's in Acuña."

"He's ignoring my messages."

"He's probably out of range." Isabel pulled out a chair and sat down. "*Bienvenidos a la frontera.* Is there a problem?"

"Is there a problem?" I wanted to laugh hysterically. I bit my lip and filled her in briefly.

"Hijole," she said, glancing at her watch. "OK, you need to cross the bridge before everyone quits work. Otherwise you'll go crazy. It's like a war zone on the other side. Crawling with Mexican military. Rory's with my daughter, Teresita. She's taking care of my niece's kids. Here, I'll give you directions." She picked up one of the daily menus and drew a map for me on the back, with a couple of cell phone numbers.

I told her I had GPS but she said, "Yeah right. I know the short cuts. It doesn't."

I began wolfing down the tamales. Delicious.

Isabel glanced out of the window. "That's your *sports* car?

"It's a rental," I nodded.

"Oh, baby. They don't cover you for insurance once you cross the Border. Those rental companies hear Mexico, they hear auto theft. A sports car? That hot?"

"Shit. I didn't think of that," I said, reaching for my tea. "I'll pick up a cab."

"No way." Isabel fished keys out of her pocket and slid them across the table. "Take my van with Del Rio plates and special window stickers so you can cross over without being delayed in either direction. You'll feel safer on the other side."

I started to protest but she waved away my words. "We'll swap keys. It's that easy. My cell phone number's on the menu. Use my van as long as you like. I've always wanted to burn up Highway 90 in a hot sports car!"

"But you're not on my rental agreement. What happens if you get pulled over?"

"I've talked my way out of worse situations." She smiled as I gave her my keys." Text when you plan to return to Del Rio, OK?"

CHAPTER 5

So I backed Isabel's blue van out of the parking lot wondering whether she had been one of my brother's many squeezes. One of those who remained good friends with him years after both moved on to other love interests. Hugh had a knack for maintaining global friends, especially those who provided ongoing contacts for his stories. He also had a knack for collecting goofballs who supplied him with information. No doubt Isabel was an excellent resource with an ear close to the ground on both sides of the Rio Grande.

I appreciated her instant response. Toward Del Rio, acres of scrubland leading to and beyond the Border stretched as far as the eye could see. I thought of those families who attempted to cross this relentless landscape illegally after selling everything they owned to unscrupulous coyotes. The unlucky ones drowned in the river or wandered in circles for days, half crazed from dehydration. Just the vast distances in this area were a challenge, including miles of dead zones.

I checked my rearview mirror for patrol cars and accelerated beyond the speed limit, anxious to get to the bridge as quickly as possible. Ahead, motel signs, factories and warehouses replaced scrubland as I approached Del Rio. As I followed the signs for the historic district and the bridge, I noticed that the grand old fire station had been converted into an art gallery.

Halloween pumpkin posters were juxtaposed with posters of cheerfully painted skeletons announcing *El Día de los Muertos.* Local families had been preparing colorful festivals and feasts to honor loved ones buried in the cemeteries.

Both events were celebrated with gusto throughout the border states. I shuddered, remembering my assumption about the murdered youth's being some sort of grisly Halloween joke. I felt a pang of concern, thinking about him, wondering if Zuniga had been able to ID him and inform his family.

I quelled my thoughts by concentrating on the route. Numerous storefronts, offering everything from cash loans to the services of bail bondsmen, brought *la frontera's* tough daily realities into sharp relief. There was even a gun shop nearby the courthouse. I slowed down. A bus from the marshal's department rumbled by me and screeched to a halt.

Grand old mansions along magnolia-lined avenues spoke of a wealthier past when sheep-ranching families dominated this part of the Border. As I approached the bridge I was glad I had accepted Isabel's van.

After I joined the line of cars, the Mexican official on the other side nodded at my window sticker and waved me on past a line of military vehicles.

I glanced in my rearview mirror and noticed he gestured to the taxi behind me to pull over.

Smaller Border towns like Ciudad Acuña, as Isabel explained, were still easier to cross with the right plates and stickers, unlike the massively crowded El Paso/Juarez crossing farther northwest. Once associated with drug cartels and mass murders, Juarez' crime record was slowing down. Or, as Hugh had said, drug and human trafficking was just moving to less conspicuous Border towns.

In softer ways, smaller towns on either side of the Rio Grande hummed to similar rhythms. People walked, cycled or drove back and forth each day to work, or to visit families *al otro lado*, as easily as they moved fluidly between Spanish and English and both cultures.

But there was also a glaring difference, I reminded myself as I drove on. Border towns on the Mexican side catered mainly to tourist traffic, including visitors seeking cheaper deals in the *farmacias* and a way to get the "morning after" pill without a prescription.

Gift shops lined the main street after the bridge, selling everything from hand-carved furniture to colorful local ceramics and wooden toys. Noisy bars with long deep interiors were lit up in flamingo pink and Day-Glo green. As Hugh once said, *"Mexico provides America with dangers, thrills, contraband and cheap labor. Anglos drive over the Border to do things they'd never dream of doing at home."* Except that the touristy shops and bars seemed emptier than usual. Sadly, Border violence and kidnappings had scared away hundreds of the usual thrill seekers, bargain hunters and visitors. Hopeful store owners and barkeepers stood in their doorways trying to encourage a few passersby to walk inside.

I pulled into a parking space to double-check Isabel's little map.

Reality hit me a couple of blocks later: broken sidewalks, ragged kids selling cheap items, vendors hawking everything from cotton candy to plastic flowers and used household items.

I moved slowly, fearful of blowing a tire in a pothole or killing a stray dog. I reached a tree-lined plaza crisscrossed by families you don't see in tourist bars. Like plazas in many Mexican cities, this was where the old met to chat and read their newspapers and the young met to parade, especially on Saturday evenings. People were busily decorating the plaza with clusters of paper flowers and streamers and gaudy altars for *El Día de los Muertos.* Two bands practiced opposite each other.

Young men in jeans and pointed boots scuffled together or hung out in one corner. Young women—with bouncy, shoulder-length hair, colorful tops and tight pants—hung out nearby. Glances darted back and forth. The plaza vibrated with musicians, dancing kids, town gossips and roving hustlers.

Isabel's little map told me to drive past the church on the left and take the second right after the plaza. *"You can't miss the pink house with the huge bougainvillea vines halfway down the block."* She was right. They were in full bloom, an intoxicatingly deep rose, giving the house total privacy from the street. I parked and climbed out to ring the bell outside the tall metal security gates.

Nobody appeared. I rang again. Another five minutes went by. Finally a beautiful young woman with glossy black hair down to her waistline appeared at the door holding a cell phone to her ear. It wasn't hard to spot the resemblance.

Teresita squinted at her mother's van and waved at me. She pressed a button and the gate sprung open.

"I'm Rory's aunt." I said, walking toward her.

"I know." She smiled, calling to Rory over her shoulder.

He appeared beside her, visibly drunk, and wearing a peacock turquoise silk shirt open to his navel. He slouched against the door. "*Jezuz.* You never let go, do you, Buzz?"

I stared at him. Now I understood the meaning of the stains and soiled T-shirt in his apartment. Not only was his tawny hair dyed pitch black. But his former thatch was cropped close to his head.

He looked uncannily like a younger version of Hugh.

Rory stood back unsteadily to let me in. He made no secret of his annoyance.

I ignored his comments about "space and privacy" and "his aunt fucking stalking him," and told him we had to talk.

About a dozen kids were in the main room steeplechasing one another over couches and chairs. Teresita clapped her hands and ordered them to cool it and go take their games to the backyard. She apologized for the noise, told us she was taking care of half the block along with her cousin's kids. They formed a mock train and jostled out. Teresita rolled her eyes and offered us coffee. Loud shrieks could be heard outside.

Rory stood with his back to me at the window, one arm propped against the frame. He rubbed his hair self-consciously. "Don't ask, OK?" he said.

I wanted to kill him. I sat in silence for a moment to take in the room. It was painted yellow, full of beautifully woven textiles and colorful paintings, books scattered around wooden bowls of fruit and flowers. Everything was comfortably untidy and well used to a bunch of rowdy kids. It was like a balm. I sank into a couch and described the beheaded victim.

He started to laugh. "Heads up, Buzz. Two heads are better than one," he slurred. "Someone give you a head start?"

Then, extending his hand dramatically as though holding a skull, he began quoting Hamlet in an exaggerated British accent, *"Alas, poor Yorick! I knew him, Horatio: a fellow of infinite jest, of most excellent fancy. . . ."*

I rose, tapped through to the pic of the severed head on my cell phone and held it up.

Rory took it and enlarged the image. "Oh *fuck.* I thought you were bullshitting me. It's … that's … *oh fuck.*"

"What?"

He clapped a hand over his mouth, threw the phone down and ran from the room. The sound of a coffee grinder in the kitchen barely drowned out the noise from the bathroom. He returned in a clean sweatshirt, wiping his face with a wet towel. "Oh *Jee-zuz.* I'm sorry. I'm so sorry . . ." he mumbled.

Before I could say anything, Teresita appeared with a pot of coffee, two ceramic mugs, a matching jug of cream and sugar bowl. She took one look at Rory, said, "Whoa" and ran out of the room. She returned in minutes with a pitcher of iced water, lemon slices, and glasses.

She swapped his wet towel for a clean one, gave me a sympathetic nod and left us alone.

"You have good friends in Isabel and Teresita," I said, trying to sound calm. I poured water for Rory and helped myself to coffee.

"Buzz, I need more than good friends right now. I … oh shit … I mean … his name's … he's known as … Al. Um, Alejandro something Sanchez."

I couldn't believe what I was hearing. "Rory I'll call the detective in Austin—"

"*No! Not right now.* Buzz, just listen to me."

I heard the panic in his voice. I waited as he rinsed his mouth with water and sucked a lemon slice.

"Al's … homeless, OK?" Rory began, still refusing to make eye contact with me. "He crashes in church shelters. He's … he was … a small-bit hustler who worked the Border."

"And you know him … how?"

"Buzz, um … It's … one of Dad's … gofers. You know what Dad was like, collecting oddballs and losers all over the goddamn world to dig out street gossip."

I picked up my phone, studied the image and waited for Rory to continue.

"Dad asked us to check out a local rumor about a *maquiladora* assembling computer parts near here. Labor conditions suck. Dad said Al moved around the Border faster than a roadrunner. God, I feel like shit! This is all my fault."

I stared at my nephew. All swagger had gone. He sat crumpled over, covering his face with the clean towel. I knew about my brother's habit of picking up grifters and street people as informers. I'd find characters curled around cushions on his sofa, or rolled up in a rug fast asleep on the floor. Folks on the run, folks seeking asylum. Hugh wasn't altruistic, he just used any and every resource. "You let the poor kid stay in your apartment?" I asked, remembering the mess and scuzzy sneakers by the front door.

"Buzz, I can't expect you to understand."

"Try me."

He draped the towel over his knees and held the pitcher of iced water against his cheek. He kept his eyes shut and said, "Before Dad died, he asked me to look out for Al while we … researched a story. Like, help the kid get to Austin, let Al crash with me for a while."

"Oh, God *Almighty.* What were you researching?"

"I'm not going there, Buzz. Too complicated."

"Oh, great." I took a deep breath. "Your father told you to lend the kid your passport?"

"Huh?"

"All this hair-dyeing activity," I eyed his black crop. "You swapped IDs with the kid?"

"Buzz. Al lived rough. He hustled IDs."

"OK. Did he steal your passport or borrow it?"

"I dunno."

"Rory this is serious. If you don't have a passport, how do you intend crossing the Border into Del Rio?"

He poured himself some water, swished it around his mouth, went to the window and spat into the flower beds. "Crossing the Border isn't a problem," he said, staring at the street.

"Meaning?"

He shrugged.

If he planned to jump the Border, I didn't want to know about it.

I said, "That poor kid probably thought helping you research a story was his break in life. You must know *something* about him. Where did he live?"

"I told you. He moved around church shelters, youth shelters."

"Which shelters? What side of the Border?"

"Oh, Buzz, anywhere," Rory said impatiently.

"Any idea how old he was?"

"Like, late teens." Rory continued to refuse to make eye contact.

The more I heard, the worse I felt. I checked my watch and reached into my bag for my tablet. I accessed one of Austin's TV news websites to see if *Crime Tips* had shown a digitally cleaned-up pic of the young victim. They had.

I held it up. "Rory, you're sure this is the kid?"

"Oh, gross! *Ugh!* They made him look like a freak. His hair was black."

I copied the sketch and moved it to one of my CAD programs. "OK," I said, coloring his tawny haystack hair black.

"Bulkier, like way down over his brow," Rory mumbled, gesturing.

I reshaped the youth's hair so it tumbled over his eyebrows. "Like this?"

"Sort of."

"Body type? Tall? Short?"

"Shortish. About five two."

I looked at Rory. "That's short. Chunky? Slight?"

"Yuh, slight." Rory looked down.

"I don't know." I continued to sketch away. I was good at life drawing, having taken classes before deciding to go into architecture. I spun the tablet around. "Does this look more like the kid?"

Rory glanced at the screen and grimaced. "Slighter build, Buzz. More like . . ."

"More like what?"

"Like … slender. Yeah, that's … that's about it."

"What was the kid wearing last time you saw him?"

"Al wanted to wear … um … like … black jeans, black hoodie."

I made a few deft strokes and completed the sketch. I spun the screen around to show him. "Close enough?"

"Guess so."

I forwarded it to my own email for backup and said, "I'll also email the sketch and name to Detective Zuniga."

"Stop." Rory raised both hands. "Give me twenty-four hours."

"Rory, this is a *murder* case."

"*Twelve* hours."

"Your point being?"

Silence.

This wasn't getting us anywhere.

"Rory, if someone mistook this kid for you, by now they know they made a mistake."

"They won't find me here. Trust me, Buzz. Twelve hours."

"I don't like this."

"Buzz, I need those extra hours."

I looked around the room. "You feel safe here?"

"Dad said Isabel and Teresita would be great contacts. Offer places to crash. Teresita's an awesome resource."

I reached for my coffee and asked, "Resource for what?"

Again, total silence.

"I assume you were completing one of Hugh's stories?"

"Something like that."

"Rory, whatever you and Al discovered . . ."

"I screwed up. I'm sorry. Drop it, Buzz. I've let Dad down. I couldn't protect the kid."

"What do you mean, you've let your dad down?" My mind went into overdrive. "Grace Colvin can advise us—"

"No!" he yelled. "Can't you see I'm in deep shit? If we lawyer up right now, police'll think I killed Al."

"Don't be ridiculous, Rory. You were here last night."

I felt livid with my dead brother. He'd endangered Rory and possibly caused his little Border gofer's grisly murder.

But I also knew Hugh was hopelessly confused in his final months when cancer shattered his brain. I should have predicted he'd ask Rory to complete some haphazard story.

"Oh my God! Does your research involve that DVD snuff flick I found in your place?"

"*What?* What the hell are you talking about?"

I told him about my discovery. Rory swore he knew nothing about it.

"Al must have found that," he said. "Way to go. That kid could find white sugar in a snowstorm."

"You mean he *watched* this kind of DVD?"

Rory shook his head. "Oh no, Buzzy, no way. Jesus, no. We were digging out dirt on some … illegal Border business activity. … That's all. Don't ask."

We stopped talking as Teresita tiptoed in and turned on some table lamps. I hadn't noticed how quickly darkness was falling.

"I'm taking the neighbors' kids home," she said. "Can you guys stick around to watch Pablito and Cara till I get back? It's OK, they're cleaning up the kitchen and working on their costumes for tomorrow. Go help yourselves to *fajitas.* I fixed enough for us all."

CHAPTER 6

Later Saturday night into Sunday

I didn't relish the idea of crossing the bridge later in pitch darkness or finding some bleak motel with polyester sheets and cars thundering by through the night. I welcomed Teresita's offer of blankets and pillows to stretch out on the couch. Though exhausted and wired, I knew I had to get more details out of Rory before I fell asleep.

At least that's what I hoped.

I sensed the gravity of whatever Rory was researching and thought I'd heard the worst from Hugh about drug cartels, beheadings, Border kidnappings and shootouts.

"Buzz, that's every day," Rory said dismissively. "I'm researching something totally different. Don't assume someone butchered Al thinking it was me. Al … hustled. *Anyone* could have killed the kid. Al worked for chop shops recycling bits of stolen cars. He … he … um … he smuggled. He traded stolen IDs. Some gang member threatened to strangle him with chicken wire if he … snitched. C'mon, Buzz. Don't make me feel worse than I'm feeling right now."

I didn't respond. There had to be a reason Al was killed in front of my home. *My* home? Or Hugh McBride's *sister's* home? I asked Rory.

He shrugged. "Sometimes the kid hung around your place waiting for me. Maybe he thought I was back in town and visiting you?"

I didn't buy it. "Detective Zuniga said he was probably killed somewhere else and someone toted the head around in a cooler before positioning it in a tree opposite my deck."

"Hunh," he said.

Rory's evasive responses began to grate. I couldn't tell whether he was dancing around information because he was in too deep—or to protect himself.

"I took the DVD and hid it at my place," I said eventually.

Then, "Are you investigating some Border trade in snuff flicks? Are they linked to those earlier murders of young *maquiladora* women in Juarez?"

Rory rolled his eyes. "Dumb questions, Buzz. How the *hell* would I know?"

Rory and I continued sparring deep into the night. He wouldn't share the extent of Hugh's research except to drop hints about some "multimillion-dollar Border resort deal" used to "launder" profits. Nor would he tell me Al's exact role beyond "crisscrossing the Border to pick up info."

When Rory mentioned "resort," I suddenly recalled the binder I noticed on his desk with printouts of land development proposals in the Rio de la Luna area. I asked if this was the "Border resort deal". He made a dismissive comment about the binder holding "that and some other Mickey Mouse" deal but refused to go into details. I no longer knew what to believe.

By one a.m. we were talking in circles. He must have tiptoed out at some point when I nodded off.

Rory was gone by the time I woke up around 7.30 am to the fragrance of bread being baked. All he did was text *"Cant quit now. In 2 far. Trust me. C U in Austin ASAP."* There was nothing I could do except head for a shower.

Teresita tossed together scrambled eggs, tomatoes and hot chilies, served along with warm, orange flavored *pan de muertos* decorated with meringue for the feast, and a freshly brewed Mexican dark roast coffee. Pablito and Cara were up, excitedly trying on their costumes and painting their faces for the procession to the cemeteries later. Teresita told me Rory had gone to shoot some footage at one of the *colonias,* a makeshift shantytown shaped out of scrap materials by factory workers from impoverished areas, many from southern Mexico. "Multinational companies entice them here, pay five dollars a day to assemble computer or auto parts. Then threaten or fire workers who get active in unions like the national *Los Mineros* or the progressive women-run local CFO. Shitty deal, right?"

I knew about the independent Mexican mine and metal workers union supported by the United Steelworkers. Teresita described the CFO's campaign against sexual harassment used by factory foreman to control women workers. I knew Rory's research went beyond workers' rights campaigns if Al's violent end was prompted by his snooping and crisscrossing the Border "faster than a roadrunner."

Teresita must have sensed my concern. "It's the *Border,*" she said, as though that explained everything. She was like her mother. No small talk.

After a noisy breakfast with the kids, I asked if I could use the main room to work.

"Sure." She glanced at her watch. "Don't forget the procession, so the bridge'll be real busy later. I spoke to Mom. She said call or text her when you cross over. She'll meet you on the other side to swap cars."

I told her how much I appreciated their support.

"Hey, no problem." She smiled.

I googled Austin TV news channels and reports in the *Austin American-Statesman,* and saw clips of my home still surrounded by gawkers. I also reexamined the victim's pic on *Crime Tips* compared with my own version. Al's softly youthful face in death was hard to match with the rough life Rory described. I felt unsettled about my promise to give Rory a twelve hour break before I contacted Zuniga and Grace.

Before leaving, I wanted to hit some of my brother's last files and reports to see whether I could ferret out the source of whatever he set in motion that prompted Al's grisly murder and Rory's enigmatic behavior

I skimmed Hugh's last interviews in Iraq and Afghanistan, vintage Hugh McBride in designer khaki, tanned good looks and black hair threaded with silver. No one would recognize the incoherent shell he became on his deathbed.

I quickly accessed his earlier reports but couldn't find anything even remotely connected to Border multinationals, property scams or workers' rights amidst some of his usual reports on crime cartels, killings in Juarez, and related police corruption. I was drawing blanks. What was I missing?

I opened his blog, amazed that some fans continued to talk to him as though refusing to believe he was dead. There was even one message from some woman trying to connect with his soul through cyberspace. Oh, *please.*

Rory had refused to close down Hugh's website, blogs or even his email connections, saying he needed all of the above for his school "research."

Damn him. I packed my tablet and prepared to leave.

When I went to say good-bye to Teresita, she asked, "*Tía* Buzz, can I call you that? Rory always talks about you as *mia tía* Buzz." she smiled. Pablito and Cara were jumping around behind her, all costumed up with white faces and eager to join the procession.

She hugged me reassuringly and said, "You don't need to worry about Rory. With that haircut and street-smart Spanish, he looks local."

I pulled away and stared at her. "So that's why he cropped and dyed his hair?"

"D'oh? I told him to go get rid of that straw thatch if he didn't want to stick out here like some doofus American college kid."

"Oh, right," I stood there wondering if my assumptions about identity swaps had been way off mark.

"You're still worried?" Teresita draped both arms reassuringly across my shoulders. "Hey, come on. I'm working with him. Rory takes his dad's piece with him everywhere. He knows how to protect himself."

"Peace? As in *paz?* You're kidding me!"

Teresita hooted with laughter. "Oh you're good, you're really good. 'Piece' as in gun! Hugh used to leave it with us."

I winced. This was information I did not need.

She paused, glanced at her watch and said, "I have an idea. Come with me and the kids in the truck. I'll take you to the worst *colonia.* Visitors only see the candy colored government units closer to the *maquilas.* Doubt if we'll catch Rory but it'll give you a snapshot of his project. I'll make this fast. OK? You have a couple hours before the bridge overloads."

"OK. Best if Rory doesn't see me—otherwise, I'll get another earful about stalking him."

"C'mon then, let's go. *Kids, in the truck. Now!*" Teresita shouted with two sharp claps.

Within minutes and well strapped in, we were bouncing over potholes at top speed. Pablito and Cara shrieked excitedly in the backseat. The roads got even worse as Teresita swung out of her neighborhood and headed toward a makeshift *colonia.* "It's not on any map," she said. "Officially it doesn't exist. Welcome to no-man's-land."

"Why didn't you let me follow you? I could have headed straight for the bridge later." I said.

She gave me a sidelong glance. "The police know Mom's car."

"Meaning?"

Teresita just smiled.

Minutes from the *colonia* we hit a dirt track rutted by tire marks. Ahead, bits of a truck poked out of the road. "Guy got stuck in the mud in the last flash flood," Teresita explained, driving around it. "Whole area turned into a toxic swamp. Dead dogs. Garbage. Raw sewage—"

"Yuck!" shouted the kids.

We rattled over wooden boards. Ahead I could see a haphazard cluster of dwellings separated by clotheslines, rock piles and a few straggly trees.

Patchwork huts of scrap metal, planks and cardboard were neighbored by a recycled rail car and a couple of cinder-block dwellings under construction.

Teresita realized I was familiar with *colonias* and shantytowns. But she wanted to show me how the dwellings encircled a single privy in a weed-tangled dip. Shaped out of planks and cardboard boxes, it stood about six feet tall with a gap of a few inches at the top under a scrap of corrugated metal for a roof. The gap provided air and an easy passage for swarms of flies. Teresita raised the truck's windows against the stench.

I scanned the area for any sign of a communal tap and couldn't spot one.

"It's on our way," Teresita explained, pointing ahead. She swung her truck around and drove about ten minutes to the nearest *maquiladora.* Picture perfect. Set in a line of palm trees surrounded by a security fence. Sprinklers soared in elegant arcs over neatly trimmed lawns. Paths encircled beds of rosebushes in full flush with the deepest of red blooms.

"At night it's floodlit," said Teresita, pointing at tall powerful lights. "And guarded 24/7," she added, nodding toward a couple of private security vehicles by the gates. "Those sons of bitches and the foremen run these places like prisons," she said. "God help workers who organize around a living wage or decent benefits. They're threatened or fired. Sexual harassment is standard fare."

We were too far away for me to read the factory sign.

"It's a European company," Teresita explained. "Some of the electronic parts assembled there might be installed in this truck," she said, tapping the steering wheel.

A security van approached.

"We're outta here." She reversed and swung back on the road, nicely paved compared with the rutted tracks of the *colonia.*

Glancing over my shoulder as the factory receded in the background, I said, "We focus on slave labor conditions in China and Bangladesh but forget our own doorstep. Free trade my ass."

"That's why we need journalism majors like Rory." She smiled.

I wasn't convinced that documenting all the contrasts here was the main purpose of Rory's quick exit earlier this morning but wasn't about to discuss that with her. I sensed Teresita thought the car ride would put my mind at rest. It didn't. I knew Rory's focus would be on whatever was going on in the executive suite of that well-manicured factory and others like it along the Border.

As the kids began to whine and agitate about being late for the procession, Teresita took several shortcuts and ignored speed limits to get us back to the house. A short time later, she pulled up next to her mother's blue van.

"Kids, five more minutes, I promise," she said, jumping out to hug me good-bye.

I waved at them over her shoulder and thanked her for all her help.

"Anytime. 24/7." She laughed. You remember your way to the bridge?"

When I returned over the bridge, there was no sign of Isabel. She texted an apology saying she'd been held up, and suggested I hang out in a fun 1950s-style soda fountain *The Emporium* on Main for thirty minutes. Instead, I decided to utilize the time to check out the source of one of the other numbers on Rory's caller ID. There was no way I could sit still.

I traced the phone number of Ruben Flores to a downtown business. After matching the time Rory had been out of Austin with the calls received and made on his home phone, I realized the Ruben Flores calls involved the kid Alejandro, or Al, and not my nephew. Rory just described him as a "hustler who worked the Border." But someone had to know more about him locally.

Ruben Flores turned out to have quite an enterprise, not far from the courthouse I'd passed the day before. A prefab shack in a bare lot offered taxi services, a phone center and a Western Union office for wiring money across *la frontera.* It was also family run I guessed from the conversation. Flores himself, a grizzled grandfather, stood behind a plywood counter switching from Spanish to English during phone calls. A surly daughter, built short and square in black leather jacket and jeans, ran a taxi service from the bare lot. Tiny grandkids were all over the floor playing with old computer printouts and Magic Markers. Marigolds surrounded a picture of an elderly woman on the counter.

I told Mr. Flores I was trying to locate anyone who knew Alejandro Sanchez, because of recent calls to this center.

"*Señora, por favor.* You know how many Sanchezes live around *la frontera?*" he said, sweeping one hand from left to right. He muttered something under his breath in Spanish about stupid *gringas* wasting his time.

I opened my tablet to my amended version of the police artist's sketch on *Crime Tips,* and placed it on the counter with a twenty-dollar bill.

He sighed the deep sigh of a man who was probably used as an information center by the entire town. "*Si.* Kid came here. Kept dropping things all over the counter. Shouted down the phone at someone he said promised to wire money here for him. Accused me of stealing it."

Flores added, "My daughter told him get the hell out. He called again last week. I told him I got nothing, *nada.* He starts yelling at me. Crazies like that? Bad for business."

"Crazies?"

"Si. Loquito." Flores tapped his forehead and waved the air, fast losing interest. He pushed the twenty-dollar bill back at me across the counter. "Why? Police looking for him?"

"He's dead," I said.

"Basta ya, papa." His daughter stood sideways in the doorway. Staring at me, she said, "We can't help you. Sorry."

I picked up my tablet and the twenty-dollar bill, stepping between the kids and the Magic Markers on the floor. Several pairs of eyes watched me leave.

I made a mental note of the address. Al Sanchez was beginning to sound like a volatile mix of hustling and hostility.

I hoped the "someone" who owed him money wasn't Rory.

Church bells peeled out.

Realizing it wasn't wise to keep on randomly trying to find out more about Sanchez, especially on a day like this, I decided to drive straight to the cafe to meet Isabel a few blocks away in the historic district.

I suddenly found myself in the middle of a marching band. Dozens of kids came flouncing along in floral skirts. They pulled mock coffins of cardboard lined with black satin. Huge paper flowers, marigolds and candles bounced along inside. Men came dancing by in black leotards marked with shimmering white skeletons.

Families in costumes and painted faces followed behind in a line of open trucks. All were en route to feast on the graves of departed loved ones in local cemeteries. The air was at once festive and somber. As I inched forward, people came streaming along the cross street going toward the bridge. I was glad I came over when I did. I called Isabel and told her where I was. She laughed and said she was also stuck in traffic a few blocks away.

"Hugh used to love this day," she said in my ear. "He told me it was like breathing inside a Frida Kahlo painting."

With one eye on the procession, I decided this was as good a moment as any to ask her how she met him.

"Years ago," she said. "Dad was in Border Patrol. He brought Hugh and little Rory home with him one night for dinner. Sometimes we babysat Rory."

I assumed that was after Penny returned to Canada.

It felt bizarre sitting there in Isabel's van, surrounded by *El Día de los Muertos* procession after the quick flip around the *colonia,* learning yet more about Hugh.

Her voice began to break up. I felt pulled back into something Hugh was trying to orchestrate through Rory, through me and through a butchered kid who hustled for him.

Out of nowhere, apparitions in frothy white skirts and white masks surrounded me. Hips twisting and gyrating, the figures moved in line to the steady beat of a dozen drums. Tall figures in red skirts and vividly painted masks wove in and out of the line, bobbing to the same drumbeat. Not a word was spoken. I stared and found myself drawn, trancelike, into their rhythm. I began to hallucinate, imagining the kid's savaged head and white mask bouncing among the dancers.

"Buzzy?"

I began to feel claustrophobic. Del Rio was Hugh's beat. And now Rory's beat. Not mine. The next band totally drowned out Isabel's voice. I waited, and lowered my window so she could hear the blast of trumpets and trombones. In a way I welcomed that cacophony as it broke the repetitive trancelike beat of the drums.

Isabel yelled, *"Da-yatta-ta-ta tatta de ta. See you soon,"* and the line went silent.

Someone ran up and poked a trayload of sugar skulls at me. I shook my head and inched forward a little more. A young musician lowered his trombone and began directing people to move to the side to let me pass by.

Crowds parted in front of me. I moved on a couple of blocks and waved my thanks.

With the noise behind me I voice dialed Grace, and left a brief update. Then I called Zuniga and left a message on his voicemail to call me ASAP.

Isabel was waiting for me by the time I finally reached the *Emporium.* With the pressure of the crowds adding to my own need to return to Austin, I sensed she understood this wasn't the right moment to ask her yet more questions about Hugh. Or about Rory.

We exchanged car keys and agreed to talk during the week.

CHAPTER 7
Later on Sunday

I welcomed the open road.

On my way out of Del Rio, I passed Garcia Gas, the business I'd visited the day before, and half-wondered if it was actually one of the chop shops Al was involved in according to Rory. That would explain the owner's wariness.

As I drove along I could almost feel the twin sensations of being watched through a window by Garcia, and being watched by Flores and his tough-looking daughter in the money center, Or maybe exhaustion was catching up with me.

Hugh would have relished this range of challenges. But I wasn't Hugh. He sought the limelight. I avoided it. My architecture wasn't about spiking the skyline with some jagged creation in glass and steel. It was about adaptive reuse. About helping clients shape living and working space out of old warehouses or barns, or transforming auto shops into artists' studios. I worked within modest budgets. I took squads of students into disaster zones to help rebuild emergency housing out of anything we could salvage from the rubble. Nobody would ever associate me with Hugh. The name McBride was common enough. When Hugh died, some people actually said to me, "Hugh was *your* brother? No way!"

Well, way. Hugh initiated my nickname, Buzzy because he couldn't pronounce Elspeth as a small boy and called me Elsbuzz.

Our parents weren't exactly mainstream, and they were so ill matched they divorced before we reached our teens. We happened to be living then in our dad's hometown, Austin, after our earlier years moving between Europe and Latin America.

Brigid Flynn, our mother, was Dublin born and a college drama teacher given to sweeping around in flamboyant capes and directing outrageously modern productions of the classics. She produced *Hamlet* as a gay man. She produced *Macbeth* in an advertising agency setting, complete with corporate backstabbing and plotting. The witches conjured up jingles. Students crafted their own sets and costumes. Hugh was her pet. She embarrassed me through my high school days and we really developed a friendship only years after I completed graduate studies in architecture. I caught a flash of her the previous night, when Rory did his Hamlet impersonation, hand extended as if holding an imaginary skull.

Iain, our father, was the second generation of a pioneering family of Scottish civil engineers in the Southwest. He spent most of his life moving from project to project, finally dropping anchor in Panama. He saw himself as a Hemingway figure who bonded with other engineer expats around a fine whiskey under whirring fans in tropical bars. I was the one—and not Hugh—who loved to trot behind him on work sites, wearing my hard white hat. I loved watching him sketch arcs and swift lines, loved the way those first rough ideas took form in, say, an elegant bridge over a river or a tunnel through a mountain. Later I helped pay my way through college by building his models and helping him grapple with ever evolving interactive software, enabling him to walk through his designs and modify them at a mouse click. Later, we clashed bitterly over his involvement in copper-mining projects in Panama that disrupted indigenous villages and threatened massive pollution. "Honey, it's *progress*," he'd argue.

We also clashed bitterly over his expectations for me. Dad thought women should just be content with pretty homes and raising children. He said architecture was a total waste of time for me.

"Men will find you a threat," he once said. To which I responded, *"Dad, do you find me a threat?"* When my marriage to a fellow architect

named Graeme Stewart floundered after a few years (because all Graeme wanted to do was move to Qatar to design eye-boggling desert homes and office complexes for millionaire oil sheikhs), my father said, "Follow Graeme everywhere he goes if you want to save your marriage."

At that point I understood my mother.

We had lost both parents in the last five years.

Dad died in a mine explosion in Panama and I regretted our inability to resolve differences before his violent end. My mother dropped dead of a sudden heart attack during a rehearsal. Yes, the sort of deaths they would have chosen for themselves. Devastating for us. But I was relieved they were spared Hugh's decline and death from metastatic lung cancer.

For some reason, such thoughts ribboned through my mind as I took country roads back to Austin, avoiding the major highways. It was almost as though I needed to return to the drawing board of our family as a starting point to unravel the Hugh/Rory dynamic confronting me now. Responsibility weighed on me. I had to move fast and be selective. I couldn't just opt out of my workload and focus on these family problems indefinitely.

Needing fresh air, I rolled down both windows to catch the cross breeze and lose myself in the crystal clear day.

I tuned into a classical station on the car radio, ah, Mozart instead of the blast of trumpets in the Del Rio processions.

I couldn't feel angry with Rory for doing whatever he did to ensure Al's safe passage to Austin. Even if it meant swapping hair color with the kid and lying to me about it. At his age I would have done the same thing.

In fact my mother nearly did just that.

Not here, but in former East Berlin, about a year before the fall of the Wall, when she took a group of students to see Brecht performances at the Berliner Ensemble. Years later, on one balmy evening up on my deck, she told me about Inge, one of the directors. Inge seemed so aloof from the others, Mom sought her out. During lunch Inge admitted someone in the group was an informer for the Stasi secret police, which was why she'd chosen to remain silent during morning discussions with the students. As the alleged informer did not join them at the lunch table, Inge felt freer to talk.

Mom asked Inge if she ever thought of trying to leave for the West. "In my heart I am over the Wall," she responded.

As Mom held dual American and Irish citizenship, she offered Inge one of her passports. She was around Inge's age and had similar features. Her passport photo was awful enough to fit practically anyone with bouncy black hair. Luckily the Berlin Wall opened before Inge took that chance. My mother was one of the first people she contacted after The Wall came down.

A siren punctured my thoughts. A state trooper in a brown uniform loomed in my rearview mirror. Shit. What now? I pulled over to the side.

"Ma'am?" He approached, his face practically hidden by a huge trooper's hat and sunglasses. "You were exceeding the speed limit."

"*Speed* limit?" I said. "Is that all?"

"*Is that all?* You were driving over eighty MPH. License and registration please, ma'am?" Lantern jawed, clean shaven. No room for discussion.

I reached for my car rental agreement and license and handed it to him through the window.

He turned toward his patrol car without a word. Big wobbly ass. Lopsided walk. Probably spent too much time behind the wheel.

I watched him check my license against his computer screen. He kept glancing at me and back at the screen. Screw this. My driving record was clean.

I couldn't believe my stupidity, so absorbed by thoughts I let the smooth speed of my rental sports car run away with me.

Eventually, wobbly ass climbed out, flapping a speeding ticket against his hand. "Ms. McBride? Your home is a crime scene. It doesn't help if you leave Travis County during police investigations."

Playing the innocent card, I said, "Oh? The detective didn't tell me."

"Detective Blakey?"

"No. Detective Zuniga."

His voice heavy with patience, the trooper said, "Detective Zuniga assumed folks like you stay put during investigations. Where're you headed?"

"Austin," I said, hating the Anglo way he said *Zu-ni-ga.*

"Your reason for leaving Travis County?"

"I'm winding up my late brother's estate," I said, which wasn't too far from the truth.

Tumbleweed rolled by us in the dusty wind. Farther along a vulture swooped down on roadkill. Barbed wire marked off straggly ranchlands on either side. There wasn't another soul in sight. I wondered if I happened to be the most interesting case in the trooper's day along this bleak stretch. I held out my hand for the ticket and apologized for speeding.

Wobbly ass looked surprised. Was he expecting an argument? He paused, gave it to me and warned me to watch my speedometer. Then, tipping his hat politely, he said "You have yourself a good day, Ms. McBride. Be safe," and returned to his patrol car.

He tailed me for the next thirty miles, then vanished from my rearview mirror at a crossroads.

I kept a close eye out for speed limit signs, especially when we approached urban areas.

Zuniga called just as I approached Austin.

Needing to focus, I pulled off the road into the dirt parking lot of a farm stall piled high with corn and pumpkins.

"I see you've earned a speeding ticket." He chuckled.

"Aww, I think the trooper was bored," I shrugged. I gave Zuniga the bare details Rory shared about the victim. Just that he was one of my late brother's gofers named Al Sanchez who probably stole my nephew's passport.

"That's it? You have an address?"

"No. Kid was a hustler who moved between church shelters."

"Church shelters? Where?"

"Rory didn't know. He thought Sanchez was on the run from gangs."

Zuniga exhaled. "We need your nephew to ID the victim ASAP."

"He's on a field trip."

"Ms McBride? Stop protecting him."

"I'm not. You know how to control a twenty-one year old with an attitude? Trust me Detective. I'll bring Rory to the M.E's soon as he returns to Austin."

I sat in silence for a moment. Folks loaded boxes of corn, potatoes, and tomatoes into the car next to me.

I wanted such normalcy to return to my own life. Instead I heard myself tell Zuniga I had amended the kid's sketch with Rory's help. Reaching for my tablet, I forwarded the sketch to him for the media. By now I knew I had given Rory several hours more than the twelve hour gap he requested. I also suggested the police sketch artist might like to redo the kid's image as I had done, showing wavy black hair swept across his forehead.

Zuniga thanked me for my sleuthing and creativity. He said they would update the sketch for the media until Rory - or someone - gave a positive ID. Meanwhile he'd run the victim's name through the system. However, he added, "If the kid hung out with gangs, no one's going to respond to *Crime Tips.* Or anything we run on Spanish channels. But we'll keep the image rolling a couple days."

He confirmed that no other body parts had turned up yet. And no missing person report. They were trying to match murders with a similar M.O. Researching an ID without fingerprints was a challenge. But, he told me, the crime lab was testing the kid's DNA, and checking fingerprints and bits of chewing gum found on the passport.

Which told me they didn't have much.

I had to go. "Detective, are cops still around the crime scene? "

"Sure. *No hay camino mas seguro que el eue acaban de robar,*" he said. "You don't need to be afraid in your home."

I knew the expression. It meant no road was safer than one just robbed. Or in my case, no scene was safer than a murder scene. I didn't find that very comforting.

CHAPTER 8

Grace called as I headed toward Austin. "Wing it here before you go home. Am I tired of hearing about you on the news or what?"

Grace lived on two floors above a downtown art museum in a 1920s limestone brick building I converted on a corner of Congress Avenue. I arranged for the rental company to collect the car there so I could walk home later along the hiking path surrounding Lady Bird Lake. Downtown was pleasantly empty. The *Día de los Muertos* procession from east Austin to the nearby *Mexic-Arte* Museum was over.

I welcomed a chance to vent to Grace outside the confines of her office. Grace was both a good friend and a good lawyer. Always quick to refer me to colleagues if she felt I needed extra counsel.

She sat elegantly draped over one of her armchairs, long thin legs dangling to the floor, fingers steepled against her lips. Her living space was sparely furnished. African and African American art dominated the walls. Her chairs and sofa were covered in beautifully woven textiles. She kept the original floors bare and highly polished. Since this was a corner building she enjoyed front and side window views all the way to the pink granite Capitol at the top of Congress Avenue to her right. Lady Bird Lake and Ann W. Richards Congress Avenue Bridge lay to her left. Powerful Texas women as landmarks!

Grace had placed a tray of fruit tea and fresh mango slices on a low table between us next to an arched blue ceramic object my brother Hugh used as a paperweight. He gave it to her before he died.

I touched it. To my embarrassment, my eyes filled with tears. "Wow. Sorry."

Grace waved away my apologies. "Buzzy, it's OK to let go. You've been thrown some low balls. I know Rory's behavior doesn't help. It sucks."

"Hugh didn't share everything with me, even when he was terminally ill. Did you know he was investigating some shady property deal involving Border businessmen before he died? And got Rory involved?"

Grace rolled her eyes. "Honey, at the end he was Bugs Bunny one day. St Francis the next. Investigating? Or hallucinating?"

"I don't know, Grace. What if he pissed off someone who planned to behead Rory and hit that poor kid by mistake? Or what if the kid pissed off someone while digging up dirt for Rory?"

"Buzz, quit. Don't let your thoughts run havoc. The kid's death is tragic. But so are thousands of unnecessary murders ping-ponging their way around the Border as we talk. We can't *assume* anything!" Grace watched me for a moment, then said, "Quick. Off the top of your head. Itemize the most important facts you learned in the last two days."

"My nephew's in danger. He's armed. I hate that. His good friends at the Border try to tell me he's just documenting workers' shitty conditions. Yeah, right."

Then I told her about my runaround with Teresita. "I think Rory's obsessed with trying to prove or complete something Hugh started."

"Buzzy?"

"What?"

"Switch roles. You're twenty-one and hell-bent on a research project. Your aunt tells you to quit because it's dangerous. What's your reaction?"

"I'd tell her. Get the fuck out of my life."

Grace threw back her head and laughed, showing rows of perfectly white teeth. "I rest my case. Stop fussing. Let Rory deal with this. Focus on your own skills. Go through Hugh's laptop. See what jumps out. Cross-reference anything unusual. I'll handle Zuniga."

When Grace got into her staccato style, there was no point arguing with her. I had to laugh along with her, realizing how easy it had been for her to add a dash of reality.

"Christ. I needed that," I admitted.

Because she was still wrapping up Hugh's estate I asked her to double-check his recent investments or divestments with a fresh eye, especially any business deals involving multinationals operating at the Border. I was beginning to sense Hugh had uncovered something outside of his reports and quite by chance. Before he started rolling into hallucinations. Otherwise, why pass the task to his son and not to one of his grizzled colleagues in the media? And why exclude me?

My cell phone chirped. It was Zuniga. One of Rory's neighbors had just contacted campus police. My nephew's apartment had been trashed, floorboards ripped up and Sheetrock axed. I knew why immediately.

"I'll go with you," said Grace, swinging her legs to the floor.

I prepared myself for the worst.

I'd waded through the aftermath of hurricanes and earthquakes. But nothing as personal as this.

"Trashed" was a euphemism. Crime-scene techs were just finishing bagging evidence, dusting for fingerprints and taking photographs. I recognized one of them from two nights ago. No Halloween jokes this time. He asked if I could salvage any object that might have my nephew's DNA and fingerprints to isolate it from whatever trace the perps left. After an OK from Grace, I stepped over rubble into the bathroom, remembering the clumps of Rory's tawny hair clogging the sink. The tech tweezered and bagged it. He found more hair caught in a pair of scissors, also duly bagged for prints. As I had been in the apartment the day before, I let the tech swab my cheek for DNA crossmatch with my nephew, and use a mobile device to scan my fingerprints. Then we were left alone with a uniformed cop and Zuniga.

Chunks of Sheetrock had been hacked out of the walls. Clothing, underwear, socks, books, files and papers were strewn everywhere. Drawers had been pulled out and emptied. Kitchen cabinets had been yanked off their sockets.

The fridge door hung off its hinges. Contents lay scattered about in pools of water and milk.

I raised my tablet and began quietly videoing the mess from room to room.

There was an overwhelming stink of feces. Crime-scene techs had scraped the sheets into paper containers but the stench still hung in the air.

Grace held her nose and said, “Thanks for the calling card. Guess whoever dumped was too dumb to realize they left their DNA.”

We picked our way over shards of glass, CDs, DVDs, dishes, files, clothes and books. Even the TV and computer tower (inherited from Hugh) had been smashed open. Bits lay scattered on the floor. I was quick to notice Rory’s hard drive was missing.

I glanced at Zuniga and said, “Detective, don’t quote poetry about a robbed street being the safest.”

“We’ve collected items for traces of drugs,” he said, peering into a hole in the Sheetrock and ignoring my comment. “Someone was determined to find whatever your nephew stashed away.”

“It wasn’t drugs. I know my nephew, Detective.”

“Oh, right. Where is he?”

“My client’s doing her best to persuade him to return to Austin,” Grace replied.

I turned away, and texted Rory again.

I then left a cryptic message on *Leaves*, the social networking site he used most frequently. As a precaution, I also texted Isabel and Teresita. I then called our insurance agent and Rory’s apartment management office.

The uniformed cop approached and introduced us to Rory’s neighbor— a fellow student— who first reported the break-in.

“You mean you guys didn’t *hear* anything?” Zuniga said, lifting a T-shirt out of a shattered mirror with the tip of his boot.

The student, unshaven and bleary eyed, squinted at the floor and shrugged. He mumbled something about “a coupla loud Halloween parties.”

“You guys partied through the weekend?” Zuniga asked. “How about uninvited guests?”

"Costumed freaks could run around the stairs toting axes without anyone noticing."

"Oh spare me," I said in disgust. "You mean you and your buddies were too wasted to notice anything."

He blinked at me and said, "Hey, I'm the dude who reported this. Get off my back! Why not ask your nephew about the fucking weirdos who use his place all the time?"

Zuniga raised both hands. "Enough!."

"Buzz, let's step outside." Grace nodded toward the door.

She followed me downstairs and suggested a quick cappuccino at the nearby *Medici* coffee shop.

"I'd puke," I said. "I can't understand how this happened. Zuniga told me patrol cars were keeping an eye on Rory's place."

Grace said, "Yeah, spot checks. Not 24/7 stakeouts, Buzz. Only a hired security service is going to do any serious monitoring. Any response from Rory?"

I checked and shook my head. But someone had added to my message on *Leaves. "Dude, yr place is totally trashed. Where the fuck R U?"* It was signed *"Corndog."*

Rory's street was festooned with Halloween debris. Paper streamers, deflated plastic skeletons and ghost sheets dangled off trees. We stepped around a compote of smashed pumpkins, candy wraps from trick-or-treaters and beer cans.

Scraping gum off her boot on the edge of the sidewalk, Grace asked, "Did you know any of the lowlifes who hung out in Rory's apartment?"

"No, Grace. But they weren't after drugs. I suspect they were after a snuff flick." Glancing around to make sure we weren't being overheard, I told her about the DVD I'd lifted the day before.

"Say *what?* You didn't think to share this with me earlier?"

"I forgot," I admitted.

"Forgot? *Hello?* What message aren't you getting about what's going on here, girl?"

"OK, Grace. I blew it."

Reaching for her cell phone, she said, "I'll tell Zuniga I'm taking you home. He can update us later. He'll seal Rory's door—don't worry."

I hesitated, remembering that binder with property info that could be linked to the money laundering Rory claimed to be investigating. I told Grace I wanted to go back inside.

"Dig around in that shit? Honey, Zuniga won't let you remove *dust bunnies* up there until he says so. It's a crime scene!" Grace said, her voice rising an octave.

CHAPTER 9
Sunday Eve

In spite of the notched-up media presence, I was glad to be home. TV vans, cameramen and curious onlookers cluttered my street. All of which probably quadrupled the *Jumping Bean's* business.

A cheerful sign read *Hours extended from 6 a.m. to midnight. Breakfast tacos served all day.*

Grace said, "Get used to it, Buzzy. There's nowhere to hide. I'll go make a statement later. You have a dark French roast for me? If not I'm joining them," she jerked a thumb in the *Bean's* direction. As a camera crew approached, she hung out of the window of her Mustang and said, "Grace Colvin. The McBrides' lawyer. We're working on a statement." She swung the car around and parked outside my front door so I could jump inside.

I dropped my sports bag by the stairs and went to grind beans. I placed mugs and cream on the mesquite bar. As French roast dripped and filled our nostrils with a comforting smell, I wondered why my work space had seemed more important to protect than my own home. I had forgotten to activate my alarm system, something I never forgot to do when I locked up my architectural practice. Two mottled ginger-and-black fur balls appeared from nowhere and wound themselves around me, purring loudly. I sensed the cats were as unsettled as I was by the noise outside.

Grace slung her legs around a tall stool at the bar, boots pointed down. "Morris and Floris missed you huh?"

"Doris and Horis."

Grace rolled her eyes, reached for a mug, and said, "Like it or not, Mizz Buzz, we're gonna watch that DVD. Could be evidence in a murder. And the break-in."

I admitted it was hard for me to pass the DVD to Zuniga before I squared things with Rory. Grace made it clear we might not have the luxury of choice.

"Grace, I need to warn you. It's sickening," I said, patting deep under the bar for my secret hiding place.

"Quit stalling, Buzz." Grace reached for the coffeepot and cream and poured for us both, checking to see "our coffee isn't floating with cat hair.".

Before playing the DVD on the computer (so I could fast-forward, freeze, enlarge or shrink specific images), I glanced outside to make sure no one was in front of my windows, and there were no reflecting surfaces behind us. Fortunately, the crowds were on the other side of my home. I had rolled the blinds down those windows before I left Austin.

As the video started, Grace noticed my expression, and said, "Buzz, focus on the perps and any clues re IDs. You recognize the setting?"

"Scrubland. Could be anywhere around the Border I just visited." I shrugged.

The gang rape started. Blood spurted on the lens, which was where I had ejected the DVD on first viewing. Someone wiped the lens hastily with a cloth. Everything went black for a moment.

"Grace, I think that's it," I said, reaching down to eject it.

"Wait." She pointed at the screen.

Blackness gave way to some hazy, shaky frames. I dreaded this.

Guys took turns, sometimes three at once, rolling her around to access her vagina, anus and mouth, though her face was blocked by male figures jack-rabbiting on and off her.

The more she struggled, twisted and turned, the more of them held her down. The lack of sound was grotesque.

I raised both my hands to try to block her image, to concentrate on the tattoos of the attackers and the make and plates of the car off to the side. Headlights beamed on the attack. Dark shapes fought violently in the background. The image was fuzzy. A kid seemed to be fighting the others, kicking and punching wildly. Totally out of control. Cursing, I fiddled with the image and backtracked a couple of frames. "Grace, bear with me," I said, inching the frames forward. I began to wonder if the kid was actually fighting the others to *stop* the rape, not join it.

Mug in hand, elbows propped on the bar counter, Grace asked, "Your point being?"

"I need a clearer shot of that background action," I said.

Pairs of hands yanked up the kid's feet and dragged him to the side. He twisted and turned to try to break free, in a bizarre counterpoint to the rape scene in the foreground. I froze the frame and zoomed in for a close-up.

"Save that frame, Buzz. *Look* at that tattoo!" Grace said, pointing at part of a wing and a pointed beak on one of the hands gripping the youth's feet.

I enlarged the frame for a clearer view and saved it. I reached for my tablet, accessed the quick sketch of Al I had made with Rory's help and held it up next to the frozen image on the screen.

"Grace, I think it's the same kid."

Grace's eyes moved from left to right like an umpire at a tennis match.

"Come on, Buzz. Your sketch could fit any of those kids."

I enhanced the light in the frozen frame. "I recognize those scuzzy sneakers," I added, zooming in on the kid's elevated feet. "They're at Rory's."

"Now buried under shards of glass and Sheetrock right?" Grace sucked in her breath. "What made them so special you remember them?"

"Counselor, I knew they didn't belong to my nephew. Too small. I recognize the unusual zigzag logo and scruffy look."

Grace rolled her eyes and continued to play devil's advocate. "Your honor, I believe the witness is trying to make connections between sneakers that could fit dozens of kids. Why do you assume the sneakers belong to the murdered kid? "

"Because he was staying in Rory's apartment. Rory told me the kid pissed off some criminal gang member. If my hunch is right, it could be because he tried to stop a gang rape."

"So what are you saying? He brings the DVD to Rory. The gang tracks him down, kills him, dumps the head in your tree and then trashes Rory's apartment looking for the incriminating DVD?"

"You have a better explanation?"

"OK Buzz. Unfreeze the frame. Let's get this over with."

The gang rape turned into a killing frenzy. Machetes. Knives. Fists. Bare flesh. The camerawork was so shaky it was like watching a pack of wild animals tearing a gentle fawn to pieces. Blood spurted over the attackers and across the lens.

The final frames zoomed in on the young woman's bloodied body parts, tossed amid the cacti like a skinned animal after a hunt. Guys in the background vanished. The screen went black.

Grace took a deep breath. "I didn't think I'd ever see anything worse than the shots of my lynched grandfather hanging in shreds."

We sat in silence for several long moments.

I began activating my copying software to save the DVD.

"You mean that DVD isn't encrypted?" Grace asked.

"It is, Grace. I'm using one of Hugh's systems that copy anything." I smiled. "Nothing stopped Hugh from accessing or editing info he needed."

"I didn't hear that," Grace said. "Email an attachment to my office for safekeeping." She slid off her stool, stood up and shook herself like a dog shaking off raindrops. "Rory needs to do some serious explaining before we hand a copy to Zuniga. It's evidence in one, possibly multiple murders."

"Grace, he swears he didn't know about it."

"Yeah? You believe him?"

"I did. He was evasive and defensive about everything except that."

"I'm outta here. Get some rest Buzz. I'll handle the media."

CHAPTER 10

Pre Dawn Monday

I slept so heavily that night it took time for the alarm to shake me out of my stupor.

Someone was trying to open my front door. My landline and cell phone began ringing simultaneously. It was the security company informing me there was an attempted break-in. A patrol car was on its way.

Moments later a voice shouted, "Police. Open up."

I deactivated my alarm system with the remote and peeked through the window.

Two burly cops held a hooded figure aloft. I unlocked my front door.

"Ms. McBride? He claims he's your nephew."

"He is," I said. I glanced at my watch. It was 3.47 a.m.

"Just checking," said one of the cops, raising the palm of his hand to high-five Rory. "No hard feelings, son, OK?"

Rory ignored him and walked by me toward the kitchen.

I thanked both officers, locked up and reset my alarm.

Rory stood there shivering.

I went to hug him but he took a step back.

"Nah Buzzy—I need a shower. I stink like a pole cat," he said, folding his arms and hunching over in his hoodie to avoid eye contact. "Since when do you activate your fucking alarm when you're at home?"

"Oh, just since someone stuck a head in my pecan tree."

"OK. Whatever. Any chance of a double stack of your buckwheat pancakes?"

Later, well-scrubbed and wearing a clean red sweatsuit he had left in my closet with some other belongings, Rory wolfed down pancakes and bananas smothered in dark maple syrup. Doris and Horis jumped on the bar and began licking leftover bits of pancake when he finished. I watched him stroke them lovingly. But my stomach flipped when he told me "friends" had helped him jump the Border into Del Rio.

"I didn't want hassles or delays, Buzzy," he explained, helping himself to coffee. "You know, like, questions about my passport turning up on a dead kid yadda yadda yadda and why I hadn't reported it missing."

"So it was easier to risk being picked up by Border Patrol with your 'friends'?"

"I knew we wouldn't get caught," he shrugged. "My friends are experts. . . ."

I held up my hands. "I don't want to know. Where's your car?"

"Teresita's using it. Friends drove me here."

"Rory, why're you behaving like a fugitive?"

"You want me to end up like the kid?"

"I want you to start telling the truth."

Sensor lights popped on outside. A raccoon stared at us from the bushes and scampered off toward the lake. The cats hissed in unison, tails thumping on the bar.

I got up and stretched. I felt wired but couldn't even face going up to my deck for ten minutes of fresh air. I had to get Rory's story straight. I fired questions at him.

"OK, let's try this. Hugh was researching some property syndicate money-laundering deal involving Rio de la Luna. Laundering money from what? Snuff flicks? Crime boss gangs butchering young women to feed a global snuff flick trade?"

"Buzz, I told you I don't know," Rory said irritably. "Al had something he wanted to pass on to me but I don't know what it was. We were supposed to meet *days* ago … but he never showed up. No text. No call. But Al was like that."

"I suspect he was trying to bring you this DVD," I said, patting under my bar and sliding it out. "I think someone ratted on him and smashed up your apartment looking for it. You need to watch it. See if you can ID any of the attackers. . . ."

Rory stared at the DVD. "Buzz, this has *nothing* to do with me, *nothing!*"

"I believe you Rory. But …."

"I can't watch it Buzz. Guys I don't know were in and out of my apartment. Al had my keys. It was open house."

"Trying to get this DVD to you could have cost Al his life. I think he was fighting to protect the victim."

Rory stared at his hands. A gesture I remembered so well from his childhood when he was tn something over his head.

"Rory I'm not blaming you. I'm just trying to figure out why this kid was butchered.""

Rory said nothing.

Sensing I'd done enough pushing, I reached for a bottle of fine malt whiskey from Hugh's collection, poured some slowly into two glasses and slid one across to Rory. He stared at me and downed his in an instant.

"Let's start over" I said, rolling a glass between my palms. "Why did your father ask you, and not one of his colleagues, to dig out this story?"

"Dad said I had to start handling something hot." Rory shrugged. "He laughed at my 'wuss' assignments for college."

"That's it? Don't you think your Dad was trying to complete his legacy....through you?"

Rory reached for the bottle but I placed my hands on his.

"Rory wait. Where were you supposed to dig? On the streets and *colonias* along the Border your buddy Teresita showed me?" I asked.

"Partly."

"And the other part? *Maquiladora's* multinational owners' little money-laundering operations? Property deals on the side?"

"I can't discuss it, Buzz."

"I hope you have everything backed up. Assholes swiped your hard drive," I sighed, opening the photo file. I swiveled my laptop toward him and pointed at the bits and pieces of his computer tower strewn about his desk.

"I saw the clip you sent me," he said, lowering the lid. "Everything's stored in cloud. Teresita's holding on to my laptop and camera."

"You're endangering her too?"

"She's cool. Street-smart." Rory sat back, folded his hands behind his head and stared at the ceiling.

"Did Teresita and Isabel know Al?

"Why would they?"

"Why wouldn't they know a kid who was your dad's gofer?"

"C'mon, Buzz, you think Dad invited his close friends and informers to the same parties?

"Why did Hugh—"

Rory butt in. "Buzz, quit! Dad always said Mexico supplied anything America wanted that was illegal. Drugs. Hookers. Hired killers. Guns. Undocumented workers. He just wanted to expose one tiny corner."

"Property deals funded by snuff flicks?"

"*Jezuz,* I keep telling you I don't know. Can we drop the third degree?"

"You think I'm tough? Wait till Zuniga starts asking questions. Which is why I want Grace to see you first. I'll text them in a few hours."

"Woohoo, I'm real scared. Big detectives asking questions?" Rory said, twirling his hands in the air.

Ignoring his sarcasm, I said, "For starters he'll want to know how Al got hold of your passport to cross the Border."

"I'll tell him the truth. I don't know."

"Rory, can't you show some concern for the murdered boy?"

Rory studied his reflection in the window. "Don't you think I cared about Al ?"

I sipped my whiskey. This was the first time Rory showed a glimmer of compassion. I started to say something, but he brushed me aside and reached for the bottle.

"Take it slowly," I said.

Rory raised his glass. "Help me, Dad. I'm in deep shit."

"Copy that," I said, raising my glass.

It was still pitch black outside. In another hour or so, early-morning joggers, dog walkers and cyclists would start using the trails below.

"So few people I can trust," Rory said suddenly. "You don't know who is paying off whom in the police on both sides of the Border. This property deal involves business leaders, politicians. And the Church." He paused.

"How much did your father know before he included you?"

"He knew about the Church. That's where things gets really complicated." Rory turned and looked at me. "Buzz, Dad didn't want you involved for reasons I can't—"

"Rory, get over it. I *am* involved." I checked the time. "C'mon, honey," I said, gathering the dishes. "Let's get some sleep."

CHAPTER 11

Monday morning

I dozed for a couple of hours, my legs pretzled around Horis and Doris, before calling Grace and Zuniga. Grace suggested lunch before we all headed over to the medical examiner's office to meet Zuniga. I welcomed breathing space to catch up on some of my own work and a little extra research that had been niggling. Rory slept on, oblivious. I saw no reason to wake him. I opened my laptop on the bar in full view of the crime scene still cordoned off with yellow tape.

My wonderful assistant, Carlos dos Santos, brought me up to speed and promised to filter our calls. Practically all our clients and colleagues had left voice messages or emails over the weekend showing concern about the news reports of the murder and of Rory's break-in, and offering every kind of help, from lakeside apartments for a getaway, to trauma therapists and lawyers. I'd had similar calls and emails from friends who included frozen meals in their offers of help. I emailed a generic note of appreciation to colleagues, clients and friends with a request for isolation.

Grace had turned the task of scouring Hugh's estate details over to her son, Jerome, for inconsistencies in investments and divestments. I couldn't wait that long. I had to find out for myself what my brother had been trying to hide or skirt around.

I didn't have the luxury of time.

I knew my brother only too well and knew there had to be a solid reason Rory kept on saying "Dad didn't want you involved," beyond some dumb excuse about "protecting" me. I tapped into Hugh's website once again and reviewed yet more of his famous *McBride Reports.*

The range of topics was dizzying. Everything from illegal "blood diamond" trade funding rebel armies in Sierra Leone to a hot trade in $3000 parrots that would fund warlords in Congo. He interviewed sleazy arms dealers on remote airstrips, guys who supplied militias the latest weaponry for "testing" on behalf of manufacturers.

Hugh was on the spot when mass graves were uncovered from the junta era in Argentina. He interviewed villagers in Bosnia who witnessed the genocide of Muslim men and boys. He even achieved an off-camera interview with a former Isis media expert living in London. Thigh deep in mud he interviewed Syrian refugees in Jordan and Turkey in winter.

Any past reports from the Mexico/Texas Border matched the standard fare of drive-by shootings, gang turf warfare over drugs or human smuggling, mass beheadings and body bits dumped on a busy street, army generals in the pay of the cartels and daylight assassinations of public officials.

I was just about tipping overload when one report from a decade ago caught my eye. It was headed *"Bones and Crosses."* I opened the clip. Hugh's voice-over rolled across a dusky view of a cluster of makeshift pink crosses in a bleak scrubby cemetery festooned with the paper flowers, photos, tributes and flickering candles of some previous *Día de los Muertos.*

Quick cut to the next clip. A noisy demo was in progress through the streets of Mexico City staged by Hermanas/Sisters with drums. Placards read, *400 Maquiladora Workers Raped and Dismembered at La Frontera.* Another placard read, *Who Pays Police to Look the Other Way?*

Cut to Hugh in combative but elegant style—in a cream suit and caramel-colored shirt—challenging the president of Mexico to do more to investigate the killings.

"We cannot!" the president insisted, throwing his hands up in the air. *"It's not a federal matter! But we are organizing a fund to compensate*

the families. Help pay funeral costs. We've appointed a new prosecutor to investigate charges of sloppy police work like the loss of evidence. We're doing our best."

Cut to Hugh interviewing a short stocky woman in a sculptor's splattered smock, surrounded by plaster casts. He introduces her as forensic sculptor Inez Gomez.

The interview is conducted in Spanish with an English voice-over.

Gomez: *"We find a few bones. We find tattered pieces of clothing. My job is to shape the face around the unidentified skulls."*

At this point Gomez breaks down and turns away from the camera. For a few seconds she is held in frozen frame.

Hugh's voice-over completes the script: *"One day Señora Ramirez's hands shaped a mother's worst possible nightmare, a heartbreakingly familiar face. It was her sixteen-year-old daughter, Maria Josefina, who'd been missing for months."*

The clip ended with a view of the grieving Gomez family in the cemetery and a final comment from Hugh about some "token arrest" of a deranged homeless man, which meant nothing to the families, since the killings continued.

I sat back. There was no follow-up story. But that was fairly typical of Hugh.

He always described himself as a "hit-and-run" reporter, who flew into a hot spot, completed a story in breakneck time, and flew out, leaving other reporters to fill in the blanks.

The story referred to Cuidad Juarez. There was no mention of murders in the Border area Hugh knew so well. Given the grisly and gratuitous nature of the murders, I wondered yet again if snuff flicks were involved which would explain the DVD I found in Rory's apartment.

Though no longer in the headlines, systematic killings of young *maquiladora* workers seemed to be confined to the Chihuahuan desert around Juarez. Similar to a little of the scrubland I was able to catch in the snuff flick. Except the poor quality of the DVD and shaky nighttime camerawork made it difficult to fix an exact geographic location.

I pulled up a report on those Juarez killings written by anthropologist and journalist Cecilia Balli some time ago in the June 2003 issue of *Texas Monthly.* It read, *"Do you know what happens to a human body in the desert? If it's fresh, the intestines eat themselves out. The body swells, the lungs ooze fluids through the nostrils and mouth and the decaying organs let out a cocktail of nauseating gases. Sometimes scavengers leave their mark, a gnawed leg, a missing shoulder. Eventually all that is left is a pile of white bones. But there is a cruel trick the dry weather will sometimes play on a corpse. It will dehydrate the skin before the bacteria can get to it, producing a mummy—a blackened girl with skin dry as cardboard, baring her teeth like a frightened animal. . . ."*

"Whassup, Buzzy?" Rory suddenly materialized behind me, yawning and stretching sleepily. He headed straight for the coffeepot and helped himself, then went to the fridge for cream and juice.

I minimized Balli's report and told him Grace would meet us for lunch.

"Cool. When do I get to see my fucked-over apartment?"

"This afternoon?"

"Guess I should eyeball your shots of the damage in detail to figure out crap I need to replace. Can I use your tablet?" He grabbed it off one of the bar stools.

"Sure," I said, watching as he retreated to his room with coffee, juice and tablet. I was glad he didn't seem to notice what I was researching. I exited the *Texas Monthly* site and shuffled through Hugh's website again.

I pulled up video clips of his funeral. He requested a requiem mass in St. Mary's Cathedral, even though we were both long lapsed Catholics. It was also his personal final "finger" at the Fox News station, located on the next corner. But that was Hugh, his mother's son, and always one for a dramatic show, complete with pipers in kilts. What a contrast that was to the tasteless mosaic design that made the area around the altar look more like a Turkish bath. Hugh also delivered his own eulogy, in a video he made of himself when he knew he was terminal, but before metastatic cancer ravaged his body and mind. Appropriately, he titled it *"McBride's Last Report."* He praised and thanked everyone who had played a role in his life and work. He spoke about Rory but somehow forgot to include our parents and forgot to include me, even though I took care of him in his final months. Now it looked as though I would continue to wrap up his earthly life.

I froze the frame and poured another cup of coffee. With a sudden pang, I remembered reading to Hugh in his final days as he lapsed in and out of consciousness. He asked for some of the lovely Oscar Wilde children's stories we had both loved since Mom read them to us as kids. Her Flynn family home in Dublin was close to Merrion Square, where Wilde grew up, the son of an ophthalmologist. She always liked to fantasize that the beautiful park in the middle of the Georgian square inspired the garden in Wilde's stories like *"The Selfish Giant."*

I tried to scatter my thoughts of the past by focusing once again on the funeral clip. I caught glimpses of Isabel and Teresita, with a group of friends or relatives I assumed came with them from the Border towns.

I fast forwarded through the service and eulogies and the scores of folks filing out of the cathedral, most of them totally unknown to me. I didn't pay much attention at the time; in fact, I was going through the paces like a robot that day.

But there was something about the presence of police cars parked outside the cathedral that made me take a second look. Or rather I focused on a guy in sunglasses, longhorns cap, a brown sweatshirt and khakis, moving between the TV cameras positioned across Tenth Street outside the Thomas Jefferson Rusk State Office building, scanning the crowds exiting the Cathedral. There was no mistaking those weight lifter's shoulders.

It was Detective Zuniga.

CHAPTER 12
Monday lunchtime

"Why are we wasting time outside the fucking cathedral?" Rory asked, twisting around in his seat.

"We're meeting Grace in fifteen minutes," I told him, backing my jeep into a space reserved for priests. "I'm curious about something. Wait here? Be back in a heartbeat."

I'd uploaded other funeral clips from my laptop onto my cell phone, and thumbed through to another view of folks exiting the cathedral. I crossed Tenth Street to the spot where Zuniga had paused next to the bronze eagle sculpture outside the Jefferson Rusk building that day, and angled myself to match his position. I quickly viewed some clips to examine whatever—or whoever - was in his sights. All I could see were crowd shots and folks taking selfies. Frustrated, I planned to take a closer look later, when I could review extra footage shot by Hugh's former cameraman from the network.

"Mind telling me what you're doing?" Rory asked when I returned to the jeep.

"Oh, checking one of the restoration projects," I said breezily, pointing at some scaffolding. I swung out of the priest's spot as a red-faced official came running out of the parish office. I waved at him as we left and told Rory to keep an eye open for a parking place near the Thai restaurant a couple of blocks away where we were meeting Grace.

"Since when do you work on cathedral projects?" Rory asked, looking at me sideways.

"Just curious," I replied vaguely.

Rory leaned his head against the back of the seat. "Buzzy. I know all this damage control chews up your work time."

"It's OK for a couple of days. That's why I have assistants like Carlos as backup."

"I know I can be an asshole—"

"Honey, don't go there," I said softly, ruffling his spiky hair. "We have some tough meetings ahead. OK?"

He nodded and pointed as someone exited a parking spot.

I zoomed in and handed Rory coins for the meter.

We took a corner table in an inner room in the Thai restaurant and ordered spring rolls and ginger tea while waiting for Grace.

It was hard to remain anonymous when our faces were all over the local TV news and front page of the *Austin American-Statesman*. I told Rory to "shield" himself by adopting subtle body language and avoiding eye contact with anyone. But when Grace strode in, all heads turned. Her tall willowy frame and stunning looks had that sort of effect on a crowd.

"Grace, this is impossible," I said.

She waved away my objections. "You attract more attention when you creep around. Folks'll lose interest when you act like a regular person," she added, reaching for the menu. "Good to see you, Rory. Nice haircut."

"Hey, Grace. Thanks."

We ordered a large coconut fire bowl with veggies to share.

Grace wasted no time. She paced Rory through the sort of questions Zuniga would ask and warned him not to show a glimmer of his "smart mouth" or "attitude."

"You're Hugh McBride's son and a journalism major taking risks to complete one of his stories," she reminded him. "*Item:* Prep yourself to admit you're in over your head if necessary."

"But I'm not—"

"Rory, do me a favor. Just listen to Grace," I said.

"Item Two," Grace went on. "Answer Zuniga's questions clearly and simply. I'll soon step in if you go over the top. The dead kid was one of Hugh's gofers. Period. The kid got hold of your passport. You didn't know it was missing. That's not a lie. *Item Three:* Your aunt tells me you were at the Border the night she discovered the head. *Item Four:* Can you explain that snuff flick DVD in your apartment?"

"Grace, like I told Buzz. I *don't* know about it."

"You think the victim was killed because of it? Buzz thought she could recognize—"

"Stop." Rory held up his hands. "Why can't you guys believe me when I say I *don't know?*"

"C'mon, Rory, you said Al hung out with criminal gangs," I said. "Don't you have any names? Your neighbor mentioned—"

"Oh great, I'm a dead man. Al had keys and could've used the place as a stash house like I told you, Buzz."

"Rory, no one's blaming you." Grace said.

"Oh *shit,*" he said, covering his face. "I have exams next month. I can't just drop out of school. This'll fuck up my semester!"

I leaned forward. "Rory, I'll talk to your dean. Keep telling yourself this is the sort of project none of the other students could access."

"Yeah, Buzz. Terrific. How am I supposed to study with all this going on?"

"We'll figure something out."

"Maximize this limbo," added Grace. "Hole up at Buzz's place. Write like a madman. You're Hugh's son. This could jumpstart your career!"

She paused. A young waitperson lowered a fire pot onto the middle of the table and placed a metal lid over the flames in the pot's core. As he replenished our ginger tea, we lifted our spoons and began drizzling coconut soup and veggies spiked with red chilies over our bowls of rice.

"Awesome," said Rory. "Am I tired of *fajitas,* or what?"

"Dive in, guys," Grace smiled. "We have exactly thirty minutes."

When Rory got up to use the restroom at the end of the meal, I quickly told Grace about Zuniga staking out Hugh's funeral, and showed her the clip on my cell phone.

She hooted. Once again, heads turned in our direction.

"Ms. Buzz, *everyone* and his or her sister-in-law was at Hugh's funeral. Maybe Zuniga was curious!"

"C'mon, Grace. Look at his body language!"

"Hard for a cop to look casual, even off duty."

"Yeah, right."

We stopped talking as Rory returned to the table.

I signaled for the check.

CHAPTER 13

Zuniga met us at the Travis County medical examiner's offices as planned. We parked our cars in the visitors' area. With his fresh baby face and damp curly hair, Zuniga looked as though he had just come from the gym or a dip in the freezing cold Barton Springs pool. His black shirt gripped his muscular torso like a glove.

He got us through security detail and led us to a brightly lit viewing room with a glass partition. Armed with her tablet, Grace waited in the visitors' room.

"Officially, only Mr. McBride should be allowed to view the victim. But under the circumstances . . ." Zuniga began.

"I insist on being with my nephew," I added. "It's not as though I haven't seen the victim before."

"I warn you, Ms. McBride. Post-autopsy, the victim's head looks nothing like it did in your bushes."

"We're ready, detective," I replied.

A technician wheeled in a draped, baby sized gurney on the other side of the partition.

Rory hung there, hands buried deep in his pockets, head down, shoulders hunched.

The technician waited respectfully for Rory to look up. Then, very slowly, he lowered the sheet. Al's bald stitched head lay there, white face puckered in death.

It was a shock to see the kid looking even more vulnerable and violated under neon lights than on the night I discovered his head.

"You recognize the victim?" Zuniga asked Rory.

Rory mumbled something, shaking his head as though trying to clear the image. "OK, yes for chrissakes. It's Al. Get me outta here."

I placed a protective hand on his back and asked if he needed the restroom.

"No. I need air. This place stinks."

"Sorry. It's tough ID-ing a victim," Zuniga waved at the technician to cover the head, As the baby gurney was wheeled away, Zuniga walked us to the visitors' room.

Grace glanced up.

"Can we get you a soda?" Zuniga asked Rory.

"Nuh. I'm cool."

"OK. Have a seat," said Zuniga, rolling up the sleeves of his black shirt. He placed a small recorder on the table between us. and began by listing the date, time of day, and our names, and a few preliminary questions.

"Mr. McBride, we're still exploring a possible motive linking the beheading to the attack on your apartment." When Rory didn't respond, he went on, "Anyone threaten you recently?"

"No."

"Your aunt told you we discovered your passport tangled in the victim's hair. When did you use it last?"

"I can't remember."

I started to say something but Grace stopped me. Placing a hand on Rory's arm, she said, "My client frequents the Border area because of his current research. He can't be expected to recall each and every time he crosses the bridge."

Zuniga thumbed through data on his cell phone. "it was last scanned eight days ago by passport control at the entry point on the bridge to Del Rio."

"Yeah, that sounds right."

"Was that a confirmation?"

"If you say so."

Zuniga ran through a photo file on his phone. "This is a clip from the surveillance cameras eight days ago when the passport was presented." He held up a grainy image of a youthful figure with wildly tawny hair. Zuniga said, "Do you recognize yourself?"

"Maybe."

Eyeing Rory's black crop, Zuniga said, "Come on. You know it's the victim. So you and the kid....what...just happened to swap hair colors in the last eight days?"

"No way. Friends told me I looked like a dork so I chopped off my hair and dyed it for a change. What's the big deal?"

"And then the victim...coincidentally...got hold of your passport?"

"What's your point detective?" Said Grace. "My client didn't realize his passport was missing!"

Zuniga stared at Rory and said, "When and where did you last see the victim?"

"Few days ago."

"Try again."

"Huh?"

"What makes you think it was a few days ago?"

"I'm guessing. Maybe it was longer." Rory shrugged.

"The M.E. estimates time of death five or six days ago, couple of days before the head was discovered. We suspect it was transported in some sort of cooler."

"Gross," said Rory.

"No other body parts have turned up. So we still don't know the murder location." Zuniga paused and cracked his knuckles. "Where did you say you saw the victim last?"

"He didn't say," Grace butt in. "Nice try, detective."

"We understand Sanchez was a Border resource for your late father," Zuniga persisted. "Did the victim ever mention being threatened after passing info to your father. Or to you?"

"No."

"What was the nature of the info he gave you?"

"I don't have to tell you."

"You think there's a link to your apartment break-in?"

"Detective Zuniga, my client is not a clairvoyant," Grace snapped. "If he suspected a link, he would say so."

Zuniga didn't miss a beat. "Can you think of anyone who might position the victim's head in your aunt's tree as a trophy? Revenge? Or, some sort of warning?" He persisted.

Rory looked at me. "How about your ex-husband?"

"Doubt if Graeme would ruin one of his designer suits climbing a tree," I said. "He prefers shouting matches in cafes."

Zuniga bristled as the three of us started to laugh. Staring at Rory, he said, "Describe your last meeting with Al Sanchez?"

Rory shrugged. "We hung out over breakfast tacos. That's it."

"Can anyone verify that?"

Grace kept her hand on Rory's arm. "Detective, unless you have evidence linking my client to the circumstances of the crime, he doesn't have to answer any more questions."

"And I won't," said Rory defiantly.

I stared at him, stunned. "Honey, you're not a *suspect* here," I said.

"Not another word," said Grace. "Detective, I need more time alone with my clients."

Zuniga looked at each one of us in turn and made no attempt to hide his annoyance. "I'll leave you to sort this out. Text me when you're ready," he said, switching off the recorder.

"Talk in here?" Rory said when the detective closed the door. "While that gorilla flips a switch to listen in? You guys must be kidding."

Grace rose. "Let's take this outside."

"I talk to Grace alone. Or not at all." Rory's voice was cold and clipped.

"I can't believe this," I said as we left the building.

"I don't need that gorilla to put me through the third degree," said Rory. "He gave me the creeps. I don't trust him. All pumped up ready for combat."

"Rory, for God's sake," I said. "I know this is a tough call. But - judging the guy on his *muscles?*"

Grace steered Rory to the left.

"We'll take my car," she nodded at her vintage red Mustang in the parking lot. "Buzzy, later, OK?"

I stood there watching them go.

"Ms. McBride?"

I turned around. It was Zuniga.

"You're not going with them?" he asked as Grace shot by.

"My nephew needs to be alone with our lawyer."

"He's wasting our time. Can we talk?"

"Oh. Sure." I followed him inside to the visitors' room. I didn't feel a need to explain my nephew's behavior. Zuniga had probably seen every reaction in the book after someone ID'd a murder victim.

He said, "We just got a hit off *Crime Tips* about the victim's ID after we posted your sketch. We appreciate your help. The caller confirmed the first name your nephew gave us."

"Who called you?" I frowned.

"A nun from one of the Border youth shelters."

"A nun?"

"You sound surprised. Didn't you tell me the kid frequented church shelters? The nun wants to talk to you. Kid was an orphan under her protection. Al de la Rosa."

The surname was different from the one Rory had given me, but that wasn't surprising, given the kid's record on hustling IDs.

"Talk to me? Why?"

Zuniga shrugged. "She knows you discovered the victim's head." Pausing, he added, "She told me she knew your brother, Hugh."

I felt chilled. "You have Sister's contact details?"

"Sure." He spun his cell phone toward me.

"Sister Colleen *Mahoney?* At the *Border?* I expected a Spanish name," I said.

"She's with the Dominican Order, Ms. McBride."

This was unsettling. My mother was educated by the Dominican Sisters in Dublin and sought them in every city where we happened to live. I tried to keep an impassive expression, sensing Zuniga was watching me for reactions.

The last thing I expected was a connection to an Irish nun. "Sister Colleen's the only response you've had, detective?" I asked.

"Apart from your nephew? Yes." He nodded. "She'll be here tomorrow to arrange formalities once we release … the victim. Pending discovery of other body parts."

I tapped her details into my cell phone. Addresses included both Del Rio and Acuña. Puzzled, I wondered why Rory hadn't mentioned anything about her apart from his vague comment about Al crashing in "church shelters."

Zuniga rose, and rolled his shoulders as though he needed to regain his tough detective image. I wondered if he spent his boyhood in neighborhood gyms or the Y to keep himself off the streets. Perhaps he had beefed up his appearance to avoid being bullied because of his babyish looks?

I asked him if they had any leads on the killer or killers and whether there was any evidence linking them to the guys who smashed up Rory's apartment and left that "calling card" on his bed.

"Nothing I can discuss," he said. "Except the victim isn't in any system this side of the Border. There's nothing in AFIS matching any fingerprints we lifted off your nephew's passport or the sets of fingerprints in his apartment."

His next comment caught me totally off guard.

"We ordered a rush job at the crime lab. The media's all over us claiming both crimes are linked to your brother's TV reports." Pausing, he added, "In confidence? We found traces of blood in your nephew's apartment and checked it against DNA the crime lab processed off your nephew's hair—and your swab. We had to know if the blood came from your nephew or you—or one of the perps."

"And?"

"There's a sibling DNA match to your nephew. Same father. Different mothers. It's a female. A half-sister? Your niece?"

"*What?* He doesn't have a half-sister! And I *do not* have a niece!"

Zuniga looked skeptical. "This wouldn't be the first time a child from the past suddenly reappeared to claim part of an inheritance."

"Why didn't you mention this earlier?"

"I wanted to talk to you alone."

I sat back and stared at the ceiling. The idea of some unknown offspring from one of Hugh's many global jaunts was plausible. But, breaking in to search for proof of some inheritance? The idea challenged my assumption the perps were after the snuff flick. I began to wonder if the DNA belonged to someone Rory knew and not a mysterious perp? I thought immediately of Teresita, Isabel's daughter. The idea had crossed my mind, briefly, because her age matched Hugh's time at the Border.

Also I noted Rory and Teresita had slept separately the night I stayed over in Acuña. Not that that proved anything but it struck me as unusual at the time. Yes, she could easily have been Hugh's daughter. I remembered her last words to me. '*Tia Buzz. Can* I call you that?" Was I naive or what?

Rory trusted her enough to leave his laptop, camera, and car with her.

"Blood?" I asked after a moment. "How much?"

"Traces of blood on a towel. Your family's been in the news since Hugh McBride's death. Not a word about a daughter. Only a son."

"I only know about Rory," I said honestly. I wasn't about to voice my hunch about Teresita until I spoke to Rory.

Was she in Austin with Rory during the days before he left town?

I speed-dialed both Grace and Rory but only hit voicemails.

"This is complicated. I'm sorry," Zuniga said, resting his hands on the back of his chair.

I rose, sensing he knew a lot more than he was sharing.

I paused at the door. "Detective, why did you stake out Hugh's funeral?"

He didn't miss a beat. "People of interest were there."

"Kingpins of the drug cartels?"

"You know I can't discuss this."

"And were they there?"

He held up his hand. I wasn't sure if that meant no one was there or five people "of interest" showed up, or what? "So that's why you were assigned to this case?" I asked.

His phone rang. He checked caller ID. "I need to take this," he said. "Call me when your nephew's ready to talk."

I walked out of the building texting Rory and Grace.

CHAPTER 14
Monday afternoon

I met them on the patio of the 1886 Cafe at the Driskill Hotel on Sixth Street and Brazos. Rich cattle barons once wheeled and dealed in the saloon at the end of the nineteenth century. The hotel's Romanesque revival facade towered over Austin's noisy bar and live music hub, and was the core of media activity during major elections and film festivals.

Groups of tourists crammed the tables. I heard a man coo, "Honey this was where the Bushes had their first date."

"Dad, not the Bushes. It was LBJ and *Lady Bird Johnson.* Can't you read?" A teenage daughter jabbed at a guidebook.

Her younger siblings started to giggle.

Rory inched his chair away from them and sat hunched over black coffee. Grace stood up as I arrived, quickly downed the last of what looked like a pumpkin spice latte and said, "Buzzy, I'm running late. Zuniga just called. Said you can head over to Rory's apartment to assess damage. He'll check in with us tomorrow. Rory, take it easy, kiddo."

"I'll try, Grace," he said, not looking up.

Grace hugged me good-bye and whispered, "Courage."

"Buzz, I don't feel like talking," Rory said, as Grace swept onto Sixth Street.

I ignored his request and said, "Zuniga dropped a bombshell."

"Only one?"

"Is Teresita your half-sister?" I asked point-blank.

"Huh?"

"C'mon, Rory, I have a right to know."

"So?"

"*So?* That's all you're going to say?"

Rory stared straight ahead. "Yeah, well. No big deal. Dad probably knocked up half of Del Rio."

"How long have you known?"

"I don't want to talk about it." He downed his coffee and rose, scraping back his chair. "Let's go," he said, placing dollars and coins on the table.

"Mind if I order something to drink?" I said.

He stood there and gazed vacantly at Sixth Street.

"Rory, sometimes your behavior *sucks.*"

The family at the next table looked up from their maps and stared at us.

"You have something to say?" Rory snapped at them.

This was hopeless. We left and walked to my jeep in silence. At this stage I didn't even care how many pairs of eyes followed us. We climbed in and I drove to Rory's neighborhood.

I tried to ask him more questions about Teresita, how long he'd known and so on. But he was so evasive I gave up and put it on hold.

We called the apartment's management office and arranged for Flossie Andrews to meet us. We also called the insurance agent and contacted a cleanup crew for the major task ahead.

We stopped by stores on the Drag close to the apartment to pick up empty boxes, plastic garbage bags and protective gloves to be able to sort through whatever we could salvage. While on the Drag I glanced up at the CCTV cameras at intersections and made a note to ask Zuniga if they had been monitored.

Rory broke down when we stepped into the mess. I expected rage but he stood there and sobbed. I thought my video had prepped him for the worst but underestimated this reaction.

"I miss Dad so much," he said, picking up Hugh's old gym bag. "None of this would have happened if he'd lived."

I reached out but he stepped back. "I'm OK, I'm OK," he said after a while, wiping his nose with the back of his hand. "Standing here blubbering like a baby. Jesus.H.Christ."'"

"Come on, honey, let's get cracking," I said, handing him a pair of gloves. I suggested tackling a core area first around his shattered desk, which was loaded with personal papers, schoolwork and items he inherited from Hugh.

"Forget about the kitchen and bathroom," I said, clearing a space for boxes and bags. "Nothing worth saving there anyway."

"I feel so *fucking* violated," he said, tossing textbooks into a box. "This is what I get for letting Al use my space."

"Zuniga thought the perps were hunting for drugs."

"Zuniga thinks this. Zuniga says that. I've had it with that hump."

"I'm convinced they were looking for that DVD."

Rory spun around. "You told Zuniga that?"

"Course not. So what do *you* think prompted this attack?"

"Does it matter?"

I took a deep breath, remembering the security vehicles and fences around the *maquiladora* Teresita had showed me. "Rory, did you piss off one of the foremen or security guys at a *maquiladora?* I know you're not just documenting privies."

"Al was the one who pissed them off. Not me."

"Why didn't you tell Zuniga?"

"Buzz, you just don't get it, do you?

"What about all these lowlifes your neighbor claims were in and out of this place in the last few days?"

"Which neighbor?"

"Little guy from the floor above."

"He's management's sniveling spy-poodle. Forget it."

"Rory, he reported the break-in. You aren't helping by blowing everyone off like this."

"Your point being? Oh *fuck!* Look at my *bed!*"

"Ignore it, Rory. That's a job for the clean-up crew," I said. Mercifully, the stink was less potent today. Rory turned away, lifted some ring-back folders out of the mess near his bookshelves and hurled them angrily into a box.

I stepped back and let him vent. On a larger scale in my *Architects Without Borders* activities, I'd taken students into earthquake, hurricane and flood disaster zones to work alongside locals to salvage and rebuild, not only for emergency shelter, but to help repair a sense of community. We'd experienced every range of emotion, every wail of despair, every form of explosive rage. We had seen extremes of kindness and extremes of thuggery. In a bizarre way that seemed easier than the very personal task right now.

I tried to joke about needing the hand-cranked rubble crushers from Swaziland used by locals in Haiti after the earthquake to convert into foundation material under new wooden huts. But Rory was too distraught to hear anything.

He crunched and cursed his way over broken glass and bits of Sheetrock to pick through documents, files, textbooks, DVDs, clothes, CDs and various personal items. He used his own cell phone to record and snap details. We tossed anything too damaged to save into garbage bags.

I hunted around his desk area for the binder with the Rio de La Luna property development printouts but found nothing. I asked him about it but he didn't reply. He leaned over and began shuffling through a bunch of photos.

Suddenly he straightened.

"What's wrong?" I asked.

He handed me a smeared, crumpled color print of a slim kid in torn jeans, boots, a striped shirt, and face half hidden by a cowboy hat.

"Buzz, that's Al," said Rory. "Taken a few months ago."

"Oh wow," I said, smoothing out the print on top of a book "Sad. He looked so much softer in death."

"Don't let that pose fool you, Buzz," said Rory. "Al acted tough to hide shyness."

I tried to match the image with the kid I saw fighting in the DVD and suddenly remembered the pair of scuzzy sneakers by the door. I placed the pic carefully with the others in a file folder, and dug around in the smashed sheetrock. I found the sneakers, covered in dust and broken glass.

I asked Rory if they belonged to Al. All he said was, "How the hell would I know?"

I dropped them in a bag and tossed them into one of the boxes to take home.

I turned away to scope the rooms to assess structural damage. Using a design program on my tablet, I mapped out a quick floor plan with a rough estimate of repair costs to discuss with apartment management and the insurance agents. In a bizarre way, it actually felt balancing to focus on a practical task that required my professional skills.

I told Rory how long it would take to rehab the place.

"I don't care," he said. "I can't live here again. *Gross!*"

Flossie, the apartment manager, suddenly appeared at the door, stinking of beer. Frizzy henna dyed dreadlocks stuck out of her soiled bandanna like a bunch of carrots struggling to escape. It was as much as I could do to keep a straight face while discussing ways Rory could opt out of his lease.

Flossie hummed and hawed until I assured her my studio would contract the repairs to minimize costs. I told her the insurance agents could work out a deal after we supplied all the necessary details and snapshots.

"Hey, Flossie," I said. "Once this place is renovated, you won't recognize it! You can up the rent. You'll want to move in yourself!"

"Okay, not so fast," she said. "We'll see about that when it's all done."

"C'mon, Floss," said Rory. "You guys never gave a rat's ass when we needed repairs. My aunt's an *awesome* architect. She's promising a total *makeover.* Low-VOC interior finish materials. Fancy high-tech kitchen. Floor-to-ceiling shelves. The *works!*"

"Huh?"

I butt in quickly. "Flossie, we'll be outta here real soon."

"You owe November's rent," she said, waving a finger unsteadily at Rory.

This wasn't the first time I paid his rent, so I made a quick e-transfer from my tablet.

"Done," I said, holding the screen up to her nose "You can show the apartment after Thanksgiving. Anything else?"

"Guess not." She shrugged and picked her way across the mess to the door, hands aloft as though afraid of catching something.

"Douche bag," said Rory when she was out of earshot. Fluttering his fingers above his head like her bouncing carrot locks, he mimicked her picking her way through the debris.

We both cracked up.

By early evening, Rory claimed he was beat and thought we had salvaged everything possible. It wasn't much, just a few boxes, bags and crates that fit easily into the back of my jeep. I was quick to note he included Hugh's scruffy gym bag with the old McBride tartan shirt, which had once belonged to my father.

A cleanup crew could now complete the hefty task of removing the bulk of the debris and hauling it away to the nearest dump.

On our way home, we tuned into our local NPR station, KUT, and caught the tail end of a news item:

". . . as yet unconfirmed reports of a vendetta against the late Hugh McBride's family, linking the recent murder outside Austin architect Elspeth McBride's home and the subsequent attack on her nephew Rory McBride's apartment.

"Speaking on condition of anonymity, someone close to the investigation said the botched beheading of the victim and careful positioning of the head had none of the hallmarks of recent beheadings in Border towns that typify mass revenge killings in the drug cartel turf wars."

"An hour ago, APD lead homicide detective Eddie Zuniga told KUT that the victim was known by different aliases. The victim's official name is being withheld pending further investigations."

"Shit!" Rory leaned forward to turn off the radio.

"That's why Zuniga wants to talk to Sister Colleen," I said.

"Who?"

"A Dominican nun from a shelter Al frequented. Al never mentioned her?"

"Hell, no, why would he? A friggin' *nun?*"

"She knew your dad."

"Who didn't know him?"

Then, as we pulled into my parking lot, Rory yelled, "Oh, for *fuck's* sake, look at that asshole reporter poking around your potted plants."

The media was everywhere.

Two camera crews and the "asshole" ran toward us.

Cursing, Rory reached into the back of the jeep.

As we climbed out and unpacked, reporters fired questions at us about an alleged "vendetta" against the McBrides.

Staring at the cameras over an armload of boxes, I told them truthfully I wasn't aware of any vendetta and we needed time to assess everything.

Rory held up boxes filled with books and papers and said, "This is all we've been able to salvage from my apartment. Guys, my aunt and I need some space?"

They gave us just enough pathway to get to my front door. I quickly deactivated the alarm and we went inside.

While Rory loaded the washing machine with clothes and went off to take a long hot shower, I cleared strings of voicemails and emails, including a flood of requests from new clients. Doris and Horis wound around my feet until I loaded their dishes with tinned salmon.

The news was turning me into a celebrity architect. I didn't want that. It stunned me to hear requests for my "expertise." One news report after another had included views of the historic limestone rail yard structures I'd converted into my home and nearby studio overlooking Lady Bird Lake hike-and-bike trails.

"We'd love a place *just* like yours," a woman gushed on voicemail. Some of my fellow architects needed the work more than I did so I planned to share referrals and made a note to discuss this with Carlos. I couldn't even face the thought of sitting with a new client at such a time.

Dean Fitzgerald at the school of architecture also left a message. Did I need to switch my next class, scheduled for tomorrow evening? I emailed my thanks but said I'd taken students on field trips to disaster areas and didn't feel good about letting them down because of my own family disaster!

I didn't tell her I also needed to anchor myself in my own work.

I shot off a few key emails, contacted Carlos and forwarded the rehab plans I sketched for Rory's apartment, so he could draw up estimates and contact one of our favorite builders to complete the job ASAP.

After showering off the dust and awful experience of the medical examiner's office and Rory's apartment, I started to throw together a pasta with fresh tomatoes, olives and parsley, and a crisp green salad. My fridge was beginning to look pitiful. At some time I had to think about mundane details like grocery shopping.

I knew how important it was to maintain a regular routine of daily tasks to balance the emotional toll. Especially for Rory.

After dinner, Rory hauled clothes out of the dryer, lapsed into a monosyllabic state and hunched over his cell phone or kept his face glued to the TV while switching news channels. He continued to be noncommittal about the "Teresita issue," saying "it's not a big deal, Buzz. Drop it?" Then he disappeared to his room to text or call college buddies and professors.

He made some comment about "hunting the internet" for a new apartment but we both knew he needed to lie low for the moment.

I suggested a safe haven out of Austin might be wise? —or even the possibility of an internship outside of the country, so he could continue his college assignments in a safer place? Rory didn't respond. I didn't push it.

I contemplated following up a recent Zoom meet with his mother. Penny was the Singapore bureau chief of a British media group. Rory hadn't seen her since high school and continued to blame her for leaving Hugh. We had Zoomed after Hugh's death. Now I had to wonder whether she knew anything about this mysterious half sister. It must have happened when she was still married to Hugh.

I felt tired but too restless to read or watch something mindless on TV. Around midnight I fixed myself a syrupy cup of hot chocolate and floated some button-sized marshmallows on top. I welcomed solitude, knowing the *Jumping Bean* was closed and the media had gone home for the night. Horis and Doris lay curled around each other on a cushion, like a Yin/Yang symbol.

As I stared into the inky darkness at the crime site and the outline of trees and bushes along the hike-and-bike trails, my thoughts turned once again to the victim.

NPR/KUT news mentioned a "botched beheading." As opposed to what? A beheading carried out with surgical precision? A mistake? Sure, the positioning of the head with the passport was very personal. Suggesting to me, anyway, that the individual who did this was not the killer. He—or she—cared enough to carry the head in a cooler and position it opposite my home because he—or she—wanted me to know about Al's death. And I no longer suspected Rory was the intended target. Up until this moment, I had concentrated on a motive aimed at either Hugh or Rory; it hadn't occurred to me someone just wanted *me* to investigate.

I thumbed through the photos on my cell phone and examined the images I shot at the crime scene.

The juxtaposition of the mutilated face and the white mask might appear to be a parody of *El Día de los Muertos.* But, would someone go to all that trouble just to humiliate the victim? I doubted that. I sensed the mask was an attempt to protect the face.

Whoever positioned the head like that wanted me to become personally involved. But why? I examined the touched up mug shot from *Crime Tips,* based on my version. Nothing bore any resemblance to the autopsied head with the stitched scalp.

Enough. I had to stop picturing the kid in death and violence. I went for the file folder with the photos Rory salvaged and lifted out Al's crumpled pic. I clipped it to a piece of plywood to flatten it, placed it against a cookie jar and angled a reading light to get a better view of the kid in the tough Texan attire and attitude.

As weary as I felt, I couldn't stop staring at it with a sense of sadness at the waste of this young life, compared with everything that lay before me at that age.

I wore similar gear when I wanted to act the tough Texan teenager and pretend I wasn't half Irish. My mom despaired. *"I'm not going out with you dressed like that!"* she used to say.

"Mom, I could get a hundred bucks for these torn jeans."

"Then get it and buy yourself some decent clothes. When did you last wear a frock?"

"A frock? Who the fuck talks about 'frocks' in Texas?"

Smiling, I reached for my hot chocolate.

CHAPTER 15

Pre Dawn Tuesday

I was still spinning around websites after 3 a.m, trying to connect the dots. To itemize. A beheading someone wanted me to discover. A snuff flick DVD that may have included the murdered youth in a desperate attempt to stop the gang rape. A DVD left in Rory's apartment that might or might not explain the savage break-in. The news of my brother's alleged daughter, who might or might not be Teresita. And finally some sleazy property deal near Rio de la Luna, involving Border multinationals, money laundering and the Church.

Possibles. Probables. What ifs.

All I had was a pair of scuzzy sneakers that may or may not identify the crime scene location and possible DNA of the victim.

My best route through the chaos of the past few days, including Zuniga's revelations, was to focus on Hugh's unique M.O., and my own areas of expertise. If there had been some controversial issue swirling around property, normally Hugh would have included or consulted me, especially any issue related to property in the state of Texas. I had the contacts and know-how. So I was unsettled by his evident exclusion of me around the issue of the supposed property ventures near Del Rio. Rory's evasiveness coupled with the disappearance of the binder from his desk raised even more red flags.

I googled Rio de la Luna. A number of websites popped up, covering history, Spanish legends, the Rio de la Luna preserve, purchases by the Nature Conservancy of Texas and a report on local ranchers resisting land deals sold for subdivisions. I accessed a map to find out exactly where the river rose and flowed into the Rio Grande. Curious about the origin of the name, I tapped one of the websites on local Spanish legends.

Up came a parchment scroll design, like a deed unfurled from history. I began reading about an eighteenth-century Spanish explorer named Luis Ferdinand Ortiz.

As legend would have it, Ortiz fell deeply in love with a beautiful young Indian woman who would meet him at night *"where the moon came down from the sky to splash a bowl of stones with silvery light and rise again from the earth as a crystal clear spring."*

Which explained the full name: *Rio de la Luna de la Fuente Sacrosanto,* River of the Moon of the Sacred Spring.

I contemplated an early painting of the spring. Utterly beautiful, as the legend stated, as only springs can look when they gush out of limestone. Modern photographs showed sheep grazing peacefully nearby on bushes and grass between outcrops of limestone and sandstone. Any area that had its own spring-fed river that flowed into the Rio Grande in drought-ridden West Texas was indeed sacred.

I exited the parchment and accessed the next site on history and legends. Apparently some descendants of the first Ortiz had owned land on both sides of the Rio Grande. Like many legends from *la frontera,* this one had taken on assorted forms and interpretations through the decades, depending on who told the story. And on which side of the Rio Grande! One infamous nineteenth-century saloon owner swore the family had fabricated the legend to soften the image of the original, murderous Generalissimo Ortiz, who was said to have boasted about seducing young Indian virgins from the local mission by moonlight.

Fact: A family named Ortiz was deeded sheep-ranching land on both sides of the Rio Grande by Spain. I assumed the original deeds were probably filed along with thousands of other documents from the

Spanish colonial era in Seville's famous *Archivo de Indias,* established for just that purpose by King Carlos lll in the late eighteenth century.

I continued to web-surf.

Whether Luis Ferdinand Ortiz was a love stricken poet or a scoundrel, one thing was certain. His descendants—among them Felipe, a rancher, and Pablo, a priest—were entitled to land that included the original mission directed by Padre Pablo Ortiz, as long as it was passed down to Felipe's oldest son, and then the oldest son of the son down through the generations. The boy had to be born within view of the church of that mission serving the area now dominated by Ciudad Acuña. If there was no son of a son of a son, the rich Rio de la Luna land would pass automatically to the Catholic Diocese. Remarkably, this custom survived the infamous land grabs made by Texas Rangers after Mexico lost Texas in the mid-nineteenth century. Parcels of land on both sides of the Rio Grande remained with the Ortiz family, but the land in West Texas was the richest.

I sat back for a moment, wondering how or why any of this material involved Hugh? I then accessed a website I used in my work to bring myself up to speed on local land transactions and pending deals, highlighting the area in question. All it told me was the fertile West Texas land had reverted to the Diocese some seventeen years before, when the last Ortiz, an only son with a bevy of sisters, failed to produce a male heir.

I could not imagine how the Ortiz family reacted to losing part of the land deeded in honor for nearly three centuries. Even if they retained the land on the Mexican side, they lost the most potent Rio de la Luna land bearing the legend of the original Ortiz.

All because the latest heir could not produce a son?

Modern property deals involving ranch expansion and subdivisions referred to a wider area. But they didn't touch the immediate acreage containing the sacred spring and the course of Rio de la Luna feeding the Rio Grande.

In short, the most fertile area had remained with the Ortiz family for sheep-ranching purposes until it was transferred to the Diocese. Spanish heritage, honor, a historic family name, a legend. And money. All lost over a failure to produce a son? Devastating for the family?

I had no idea what part of all of this involved the reports in the binder on Rory's desk and cursed myself for not lifting it when I had a chance.

Exhaustion hit me. I exited the historic reports and closed my laptop. I decided to grab a couple of hours' sleep, at least, before tackling the challenges of the new day. I had arranged to meet Sister Colleen Mahoney at a diner close to the medical examiner's office while Rory and Grace had their "discussion" with Detective Zuniga. I thought Sister might be as good a person as any to talk to about the original Ortiz land and whether the Diocese planned to develop it.

There was only one problem. By the time I awoke, Rory was gone. He left a brief note on my whiteboard.

Quit worrying. Returning to the Border. I texted Grace. R.

I took a deep breath and told myself I had to let him go.

I liked Sister Colleen the moment I saw her reverse a battered old Chevy truck into the diner parking lot close to the Medical Examiner's building, one hand holding the door open because her side-view mirror was shattered. She jumped out in jeans and a green sweatshirt. I joined her from the bus stop.

Had I not known she was a nun, I would have assumed she worked on a ranch. She was deeply freckled. Her curly auburn hair hugged her head like a cap. It took a stretch of the imagination to visualize her in the traditional cream-and-black Dominican habit, which she probably rarely wore.

Before I could open my mouth, she said, "Ah, I'd recognize you anywhere, Buzzy. You McBrides are hard to miss with your black hair and cornflower blue eyes. So handsome and so Black Irish looking, the pair of you!"

"You flatter us, Sister Colleen," I smiled.

"Drop the 'Sister,' would you now? Your brother always nicknamed me Irish Terrier."

She still spoke with a crisp Dublin voice, even though she told me she'd lived between Mexico and Texas over twenty years. She sounded a little like Mom and I loved that.

As we walked into the diner, I realized she'd left the Border around the same time I turned in for a couple of hours of sleep. Ironically, she probably passed Rory on the road.

We ordered a jug of freshly squeezed orange juice, a carafe of coffee, mushroom and spinach omelets, hash browns and hot biscuits.

"Grand," she said approvingly. "Could do with some hot food. This won't be the first time I've had to arrange formalities for one of our murdered kids, but I never get used to it."

I quickly brought her up to speed about discovering Al's head on Halloween night and mistaking it for the sort of props my mother used to store in the university's drama department.

"I hate to have to say this, Buzz. Al seemed destined for a violent end. Or life in prison. If he knew someone like *you* found his head . . ." Her voice trailed off. Then she launched into the work they did with homeless, orphaned or throwaway kids. Including yet more unaccompanied minors or kids who lost their parents trying to jump the Border.

" We give them a safe, clean haven, get them into schools where we can, arrange training programs in auto shops, construction, even local craft shops and with *curanderas.*"

Leaning forward, she whispered, "We're a 'sanctuary' for the undocumented and runaways, and provide legal help and contact families where necessary."

I gave her a thumbs-up, mentioned my support for sanctuary, and asked, "Have the authorities tried to close you down?"

"Over my dead body," she said. "We arrange phalanxes of folks to encircle kids to prevent ICE from scooping them up when we take them to medical appointments or asylum hearings." Pausing, she added, "I'm not slow to use Catholic guilt to encourage certain ICE agents with Irish or Spanish surnames to look the other way when necessary."

I believed her. She ate with relish. Between mouthfuls, she admitted news of Al's murder came as no surprise. "Buzzy, we did our best. Young Al was out on the street with the others as a six-year-old, sniffing glue, learning pickpocketing skills. Ah, far more exciting than sitting around with a bunch of old nuns whispering Hail Marys, wouldn't you know?"

I nodded in agreement.

"Our kids come from everywhere," she went on, waving her fork in circles. "some escaped violence or gangs as far down as El Salvador, Honduras. Others were born of local mothers forced into prostitution, or drug addicts in and out of prison. We get teenagers thrown on the streets and nowhere to go."

"I hate to think what happens to kids who *don't* find you," I said. "Any idea how my brother met Al?"

"You don't know, do you? Otherwise I wouldn't be here."

Puzzled, I shared the little I knew from Rory about Al being an orphan and a "hustler."

Colleen put down her knife and fork and fixed me with clear green eyes that matched her sweatshirt. "Hmm," she said after a while. She glanced around the busy diner and helped herself to more coffee.

I raised my eyebrows.

"We give the kids a structure," she said. "Teach them the basics. But we're no substitute for parents. Some finish high school and get into training programs. Some return to the streets. Al was … different. Gifted. Charming. But as for those criminal gangs . . ."

Her voice trailed off. I sensed she was stalling for time, trying to figure out how much I knew or didn't know, and how much she should share.

"How criminal?" I asked. "Was Al involved with one particular gang? Do you know a name? Symbols? Tattoos?" I described some fragments of the tattoos I saw in the DVD.

Colleen shrugged. "Oh, young Al used to … play around with those tattoo stickers on his arms," she smiled. "Bit of a tease, if you ask me. Dangerously so."

"Dangerously so? You believe his murder was gang related? Which gang did he piss off? Anyone linked to the *maquiladora* bully-boys?

"Ah, now, I'm not going there, Buzz. We tread a fine line in the neighborhood," she said, rolling her hands. "Part refuge. Part rehab. But we don't play sides. We can't risk being caught in crossfire."

"I understand," I said. "I'm trying to figure out if he was killed by gangs. Or if his murder was related to research he was doing for my student-journalist nephew Rory." I told her about the discovery of Rory's passport tangled in Al's hair.

"Jesus, Mary and Joseph." She looked down. "How cruel."

I could tell she was avoiding getting drawn into any comment about Al's killers so I didn't press the point.

"Our local kids are often abandoned as babies, or two-year-olds or eight-year-olds or any year olds," she said, switching suddenly to a safer topic. "Next time you hear about your friends wasting thousands of dollars on fertility treatments or surrogates, send them to me to adopt one of our kids."

"You knew Al as a *baby?*" I asked, surprised.

She nodded.

I toyed with my omelet and waited for her to continue.

"Al was one of three or four abandoned babies Hugh brought to us. He saw a young girl leave Al outside a church in Acuña. *Sin nombre.* Except the baby was wrapped in rose petals. That's why we chose the name de la Rosa."

"My nephew claimed Al's surname was Sanchez."

"Sanchez. Martinez. Gonzales. Al used different IDs to move hither and thither, I was told." She spread marmalade on her biscuit and added, "Hugh was very generous to our shelters after bringing us abandoned babies."

It made perfect sense to me that Hugh would deliver foundlings to the local Dominicans to raise, given our mother's long association with the Order. The possibility of a baby ending up like Al was almost too much to bear.

"If my brother was generous to your shelters, I will be too," I said after a moment.

"You're most kind. But there's no need. . . ."

"Oh yes, there is."

She glanced at her watch.

"Colleen, one last question?"

"Only one?" She smiled.

"It's about Diocesan land along Rio de la Luna acquired from a family called Ortiz some sixteen, seventeen years ago?"

"What about it?"

"Do you know if the Church plans to develop or sell it?"

"Ah, no. That's *not* my area of expertise." She smiled and seemed relieved, making me wonder what she thought I was about to ask. "Dioceses all over America had to sell property to pay legal costs after shielding those disgraceful pedophile priests. Ortiz land, you say?" She frowned. "I'll make one or two inquiries and call you." She reached into a back pocket for a notebook and scribbled a reminder to herself. She didn't ask why I was curious but downed her coffee, thanked me for a lovely breakfast and said, with some reluctance, "I'd best be off now to bless whatever's left of that poor child."

I paid and we walked out to the parking lot together in silence.

"Would you like me to go with you?" I asked.

Colleen shook her head, reached into the truck for a simple black veil and tossed it expertly over her auburn curls.

CHAPTER 16

I watched the nun sprint across the block toward the Medical Examiner's building. What an unlikely source of yet more puzzling sides of Hugh.

Colleen added a spin to a kaleidoscope where fragmented facts created different patterns with each turn. I toyed with the idea of heading to my studio to catch up on work. But wondered if it would be possible to concentrate on questions about design specifications to meet city codes, or sustainable solutions for an abandoned storefront conversion into an aikido dojo. Best to deal with all that tomorrow.

I called Carlos. He said no one expected me to leap into meetings or resolve problems instantly. "Take a few extra days" he added reassuringly.

It wasn't my way to have unlimited time to resolve problems. Feeling in need of the crisp fall air and exercise, I decided to hop on a bus that dropped me off close to Lady Bird Lake so I could take the hiking trail home. I was trying to avoid using my yellow jeep where possible because it was so conspicuous.

Walking helped me think. I also had to figure out a way of dealing with my brother's former media colleagues who kept requesting exclusive interviews. I was nowhere near ready for that. Pity I couldn't hand the task to Rory to give him the rare experience of being on the other side of a TV lens. If he kept up his disappearing acts I couldn't schedule him to do anything at all.

Along the trail, fall's golden and brown leaves stood out against the backdrop of a sharp blue sky.

The lake twinkled like scattered jewels through the needles of a bald cypress, just beginning to show signs of rust. It was a perfect time in Austin after the dense humidity of summer. Fall had its own lingering character in the city, with a pure quality of light beloved of artists. A palette of reds from Spanish oaks, crape myrtles, Chinese pistachios and nandinas contrasted with the browns of pecan and sycamore trees. Pecans were in abundance along the lake, gardens and avenues. Squirrels scurried to-and-fro collecting nuts from the paths. Joggers crunched discarded shells underfoot.

Since this was a weekday, the hiking trails were less crowded. I wanted to surround myself with the beauty of Austin's fall. When cold winds blasted coastal areas, seabirds flew inland to nest on Lady Bird Lake, along with the local ducks, coots, loons and long-legged white and blue herons, a sight I loved to watch from my deck. To think we had all of this in downtown Austin, a gift for city dwellers who swarmed into the new high-rises.

In January we could experience one of our famous ice storms, but spring always came early. Hugh had died in the spring and I wondered if I would relive his final weeks at the first sign of peach blossom.

As I neared my home, a sweep of black-and-orange monarch butterflies settled on the surrounding bushes, and then seemed to follow me as a guard of honor. They frolicked and darted about. Puzzled, I took snapshots on my cell phone. This was late for monarchs. Numbers were dwindling as breeding grounds were threatened by pesticides further south, so we cherished any sightings.

Austin was on the monarchs' fall migratory route down to Mexico. But traditionally, around *Dia de los Muertos,* scores soared into the sky over Angangueo, the Mexican mountain village and former silver mining area.

The monarchs hovered in midair as though waiting for me to catch up. Then they fluttered onward and spread out on lantana bushes of pincushion-like clusters of yellow and orange to match their wings.

As I got closer, they flew off toward the pink lantana bushes where

Al's head had dropped. The area was still cordoned off by crime-scene tape. It was as though a wave of them found me to remind me that during *Dia de los Muertos* over Angangueo, the butterflies confirmed an ancient Aztec inspired belief that they were the returning spirits of beloved relatives. In essence, a belief that matched the presence of departed souls at *Samhein.*

In awe, I stood and watched them for a long time. A small child pedaled up on a purple tricycle and her parents shouted, "Leanne, don't go there, Don't go there!"

With a flurry of wings, the monarchs scattered off toward the lake. The words of Federico García Lorca, the Spanish Civil War poet, filled my thoughts: *"Los esquelotos de mil mariposas duerman en mi recinto." "A thousand butterfly skeletons sleeping in my walls."*

I called Sister Colleen, hoping she was out of the medical examiner's building by now.

"It was a sad moment" was all she would say.

I told her about the butterflies.

"Wait, now," she said. "I'm just walking to my truck. Tell me more."

I described the way the monarchs followed me along the hiking trail and fanned out on the bushes where I had discovered Al's head.

"Al's way of saying goodbye," she said. Then, "Did you know butterflies used to follow St. Joan into battle?"

I didn't know that, but her voice began breaking up. I lost the connection.

I called back and left a vm saying I felt the butterflies were telling me to plant extra milkweed bushes to attract them, to honor Al's spirit.

When I got home, I found the owners of the *Jumping Bean* had left me a cheerful card. They said they knew what a hard time this was for me and what a hassle it was with the media and gawkers around my home. But, as their business had tripled, they offered me a couple of weekend brunches on the house. Perhaps I could also advise them on how to expand their patio area?

I had to smile. They were the sort of folks who added to the city's beloved slogan, *"Keep Austin Weird."*

I returned a vm from Grace, but her assistant said she was in court so I left a message for her to call whenever. Rory had worn my patience to a frazzle.

I began the sort of exercise I encouraged my students to do when their minds were tangled. Pair up and fire questions at one other. *Don't think. Speak. What images jump out?*

I asked myself the same question.

Images?

—A beheading of a kid my brother had rescued as a newborn and used as a gofer.

—Border characters like Isabel and her daughter, Teresita, who might be my niece.

—Zuniga watching a person or persons unknown at Hugh's funeral.

—Hugh's possible involvement in a mysterious Ortiz land deal involving the Rio de la Luna area and the local diocese.

—A snuff flick.

—Followed by the attack on my nephew's apartment. Connections?

I penned each item in a different color on my whiteboard, to keep on catching my eye as I moved about.

The common denominator was Hugh.

I opened my laptop, pulled up his site again and accessed his archives, articles in the print media he'd digitized from the time before he went into TV.

I knew this was a long shot. I entered the word Ortiz. Several links popped up, which didn't surprise me, since it was like looking up the name Jones or Smith. I narrowed it down to Hugh's years at the Border.

His Ortiz clips covered a lot. I skimmed through the titles and opened one headlined "Border Patrol Uncovers Grandma's Secret Smuggling Tricks."

The story was boilerplate Hugh from his early days in journalism. It read:

> *Grandma Esperanza Alvarez of Acuña was on her way to her great-grandson's first communion in Del Rio when a Border Patrol*

officer happened to notice the diminutive eighty-year-old climb out of her wheelchair and scamper up the church steps. Two burly young men then flung the wheelchair into the back of a pickup truck and drove off at great speed.

The Patrol gave chase. Shots were fired from the truck. Shots were fired back.

Then the truck hit a speed bump. Out popped Grandma's wheelchair. It came flying through the air like a missile. While police continued chasing the men in the truck, Border Patrol agents stopped traffic to retrieve Grandma's broken chair.

Its metal frame and seat did a lot more than support Grandma's "nalgas." They were filled with cocaine. Grandma's chair was worth a cool $50,000. Once caught, her grandsons Pepe and Adolfo Ortiz were discovered to be leaders of the "grandparent connection," involving groups of elderly men and women who frequently crossed the Border with illicit drugs hidden in their underwear, hats, walking sticks or wheelchairs.

It wasn't the story as much as the photograph that held my eye. The Border Patrol agent who helped track the Ortiz brothers. There she was, climbing out of the van, youthful, beautiful, athletic, unmistakable.

It was Isabel.

Stunned, I added another line to the whiteboard list and yet another question for Rory.

Back on the laptop, on a hunch I entered the names Pepe and Adolfo Ortiz in the search slot.

Up popped something else Hugh wrote following the arrest of the Ortiz brothers.

Pepe and Adolfo were suspected of murdering their cousin Jesse Felipe Ortiz, allegedly for exposing the family's involvement in the "grandparent connection" drug-smuggling enterprise. Neither was caught.

It was the next line that hit me.

Jesse Felipe Ortiz was the oldest son of the oldest son going back to the historic origin of the Ortiz land grant involving the Rio de la Luna.

The family considered him an outcast because he was solely responsible for losing the rich, sheep rearing Rio de la Luna land to the Diocese when he failed to produce a male heir. His young wife and baby daughter both died in childbirth.

That was Hugh's final report on the family.

I summarized the details, added more lines to the whiteboard and made connections with arrows to cross-match dates and events. What I really needed in that moment was one of the versatile design programs I used like Archicad, where I could enter all the relevant data and animate everything in interactive 3D with walk-throughs. At the click of a mouse I could play around with materials, dimensions and variations to enhance location compatibility in different seasons and times of the day. How simple that would be.

Instead, like someone needing memory prompts, I stared at multicolored lines on a whiteboard.

An Amtrak train clattered by outside. The noise was louder when winds blew in certain directions. Normally I enjoyed the sound as much as I loved freight trains rattling over the rusted bridge up lake, especially when they synchronized with my cathedral chimes on the deck. But right at this moment the sound grated.

I got up and stretched, then glanced back at the whiteboard. Two dates suddenly jumped out.

Hugh's final report on the Ortiz family happened just a few months before his marriage to Penny ended and he left the Border. Connection? I texted Isabel.

CHAPTER 17
Late Tuesday afternoon

I checked the local time in Singapore. It was before dawn. Perhaps a little early for Penny. No response yet from Isabel. I wondered which woman I'd reach first, and how honest each would be with me?.

I decided to keep researching items that didn't depend on a time zone at the other end of the world or someone's being out of range at the Border.

I hadn't fully explored Hugh's funeral as a resource, partly because of a resistance on my part to do more than glance through some of the clips. Now I was tempted to review the livestream to see if anything new hit me, and also to try to figure out once again who or what Zuniga was monitoring that day.

I made myself some strong Assam tea, and opened the livestream. I turned down the sound, unwilling to hear bagpipes or Monsignor O'Hare's sanctimonious voice. I reviewed the rituals and replayed sweeping views of the mourners both inside and outside the cathedral. Especially the group with Isabel and Teresita. There were more people with them in the pews I hadn't noticed earlier.

A few pews behind them sat Sister Colleen in a cream-and-black Dominican habit. Next to her sat three teenage boys. One had a thick mop of black hair hanging over his eyes. This could have been Al but I wasn't sure.

I stepped back, froze, enlarged the frame, and stepped back again to view a brief sequence in case I was jumping to conclusions.

But the kids had their heads down or leaned toward one another, so I really couldn't catch a glimpse of their faces.

I fast-forwarded to the end of the funeral mass as people began pouring out of the cathedral to a blaze of TV cameras. I caught glimpses of Rory next to me on the steps greeting friends, media and U.T. colleagues, Hugh's frat brothers, his nurses and oncologist, and our McBride cousins. My mother's family watched from the comfort of their homes in Dublin. I continued studying the crowds until I caught sight of Zuniga across the road. The view widened but it was just too dense with people and TV cameras and cop cars to see whom or what he was observing. Except I noticed he wasn't with the other cops, but walked up to the top of the steps of the Rusk building, next to the bronze eagle sculpture. Frustrated, I exited.

Then, to hell with the time difference in Singapore. I pulled up the Zoom site, and entered my contact list to access Penny's name. She appeared on my screen within seconds. Her bushy tawny hair was all tousled, reminding me of Rory's thatch before he chopped and dyed it black.

A lush tropical garden with palm trees and Birds of Paradise peeped through the window behind her in the early morning light.

Her first words were "What's wrong? Has something happened to Rory?"

I reassured her. She sat back and sighed, waiting for me to go on. We Zoomed one another some months ago when Hugh was dying, as he wanted a chance to say good-bye to her. Rory and I Zoomed her briefly after the funeral. Penny also emailed when news about the murder and the attack on Rory's apartment went viral. I left it to Rory to respond and doubted he had.

"Penny, this isn't easy for me," I admitted, swiftly bringing her up to speed. Then I added, "Maybe I misjudged you for leaving Hugh and Rory. What really happened that year?"

She stared at me. "Is Rory there?"

I shook my head.

"Whatever I tell you, stays between us."

"Always."

The image of her face began to break up on the screen like a Picasso painting. But her soft Canadian accent came through like a clear stream rippling through a forest. "Ask questions. I'll answer them honestly."

I waited until the screen adjusted itself so we were eye to eye again, "Did you quit because Hugh fathered a daughter on the side?"

"Ah, so you've discovered that."

I was stunned.

"I just found out," I said. So you knew he was involved with a Border Patrol agent named Isabel?"

Penny looked bewildered. "I knew Isabel. But she was very married at that time to another Border Patrol agent, Tony somebody-or-other. They had a baby girl. . . ."

"Teresita?"

"That's it."

"I thought Teresita was Hugh's daughter?"

Penny burst out laughing. "No way. Hugh was like a big brother to Isabel. He knew her parents well. Her dad was also in Border Patrol. Don't you remember when you joined us at their place for that *tamaladas* party?"

I told her I had a dim memory of the party.

Penny chuckled and shook her head. "Buzzy, I don't know what you've heard but Hugh didn't fool around with people who were that close. Only with those he barely knew."

"Tell me about this alleged daughter."

Penny placed both elbows on her desk. "OK," she began. "A young teenage Latina turned up on our doorstep one day with a baby in her arms, screaming, yelling at Hugh in Spanish about the baby being his. It was like some bad B movie. Hugh called Isabel's father in Border Patrol and had the girl deported."

"With the *baby?*"

"I assumed so. Hugh swore it wasn't his. I didn't believe him for a minute. He launched into some bullshit about a deal he made to do some guy a favor in exchange for an exclusive hot story. You know how he was, throwing his hands in the air, claiming everything backfired. That's all I know. "

I felt chilled. "Who was this 'guy'?"

"I have no idea, Buzz. Hugh refused to discuss it. Told me it was none of my business."

"That's why you left him?"

"Oh no. That was just the final straw."

"Tell me."

"You don't want to hear this."

"Try me."

"Hugh's idea of fun was threesomes. Didn't matter if the other party happened to be male or female. Sometimes he'd bring home anyone who was curious. He expected me to play along. I was a wild young thing until tiny Rory walked in on us one night and started screaming. That was it."

She stopped talking and looked away.

"Oh, Penny, my God," I said, remembering an incident during my own student days in spring break when I got totally wasted on a Padre Island beach after midnight with a bunch of college buddies including some of Hugh's frat brothers. As the surf broke over our naked bodies, we rolled and romped around one another, coupling, blowing, moving from muscular sets of thighs to soft thighs, laughing, not really caring who went with whom. I woke up the next morning in a clump of sea oats and couldn't even remember who I'd blown or straddled, but only remembered being thankful I was on the pill at the time. Hugh found out about the adventure and slapped me in the face for *"behaving like a slut around his frat brothers."* I went for him in a rage, accusing him of double standards. I reminded him of the day I overheard him boasting to a buddy about the time during a movie when he and another guy sat on either side of one of my friends, who was wearing a white blouse. The boys rubbed melted chocolate on their hands and fondled her breasts. When the lights went on they ran and watched as she left the cinema in tears with her arms crossed over her chocolate-smeared front. *"That was cruel, you goddamn bastard!"* I remember shouting at him.

I couldn't bring myself to share this with Penny, but nothing she told me was a surprise. All I said was "I had no illusions about Hugh."

"Too bad I didn't know that a couple of decades ago. What was it you said to me? What sort of half-assed mother was I to walk out on your brother and little Rory?"

"Penny, I am so sorry. If only you'd told me at the time?"

Penny shook her head. "Impossible. I planned to take Rory with me to Vancouver. Hugh said I was nothing but a dull prudish Canuck who couldn't turn him on unless he watched me 'perform' with others. He said if I left with Rory, he had enough contacts in the media to destroy me. Personally and professionally."

"Didn't you consult a lawyer?" I was shocked.

"Oh, *please,* Buzz. I was young, vulnerable, a Canadian citizen and totally alone in the United States. I couldn't tell my family the truth. My father was a strait-laced minister, remember?" She paused and looked away.

"I would have supported you."

"I wonder? To protect Rory I kept quiet." She added sadly, "My only option was to pack my bags and fly home."

"So Hugh could sue for divorce on the grounds of desertion?"

"Oh yeah, and have my son grow up idolizing his famous father with that wonderful TV image adored by millions. *I* was considered scum."

"Penny, all these years . . ." My voice trailed off. "I hope you can resolve things with Rory one day. He needs you right now. He's in a tailspin."

"I'm not surprised. How's he taking everything?"

"Not well. Rory's between denial and … crisis mode. He handles it by going AWOL."

Penny smiled. "He gets that from me." Breezes swayed the palm trees in the window behind her, as though nodding in agreement. "I'd do anything to help if he'd let me."

"He may need to leave the USA for a while."

"Send him to me."

"It's not that easy, Penny. He can't just free-fall through Singapore."

"I'll text him. See what I can do about hiring him as an intern."

CHAPTER 18
Tuesday eve

Students were silent when I walked into my class in the school of architecture. I eyed the rows, amazed to see triple the number that usually attended my evening electives.

I propped myself on the edge of the table on the platform, folded my arms, and said, “Does it surprise you guys to hear I couldn’t wait to see you?”

Loud cheers. High Fives.

“Thanks,” I smiled. “OK! Our theme is *Reality and Illusion in Architecture.* No power point tonight. I want your thoughts. When do we use illusion and why?”

“Trompe l’oeil,” said Bo, a slim young man in huge horn rimmed spectacles. “A fresco creating the illusion of space or an extra dimension to a room or a room leading into a room.”

“Like a painting of a window opening to a scene of rolling hills on a wall,” said Sylvie, a tall woman in fluffy scarves. “A Magritte touch. To add depth.”

“Nah. Too tame,” shrilled Jayne from the back. “I livened up my kid brother’s room after he came home from hospital by painting one dark wall with images of his friends bouncing up and down on a trampoline. It made him feel they were with him 24/7.”

"Brilliant," I said. "But is this an evolving project? Do you think your little brother may may want different images in a year?"

"Yeah, maybe *he'll* be into something tame down the line," Sylvie smiled.

"Let's change pace here, guys," I suggested. "Remember some of the Japanese styles we discussed last time? —where a bathroom opens to a beautiful garden to give you the *illusion* of bathing outdoors? Compared with most of our bathrooms, where windows are tiny or blocked to give us privacy and seclusion."

"If my bathroom opened to my yard, neighbors would be selling pay-per-view tickets," a bulky young man in a hooded Longhorn sweatshirt said from the side.

"Pay to watch *you* shower?" Yelled Bo. "Give us a break, Spider!"

Hoots of laughter.

"OK guys, let's get more colorful," I suggested tactfully. "Hundertwasser's house in Vienna makes you feel you're in a Klimt painting," I said. "Crazy mosaics, and a rolling floor underfoot. Exciting, but a challenge for wheelchairs, or anyone with balance problems."

"Or anyone in those skinny high heels," added someone in the front row.

I said, "this is cool, but I want to hear about *your* sudden flashes of inspiration. Your wild ideas. Forget other people's dazzling work for now. What have you seen *this week* that prompted a snap design solution? Come on, inspire me. Anyone?"

"I cycled by a large ground-floor space on a corner with a wrap-around window last night," a tiny voice ventured from a middle row. "Awesome place for something like a dance studio or a martial-arts dojo."

"Come closer," I said, "we can't hear you!"

Ming, a young Asian student, came trotting down and made an elegant tai-chi-like turn to face the class. "What a waste of space. It was a wallpaper showroom. Boring. I wanted *movement* in that window … like … folks swirling and sweeping around! All lit up at night for everyone to enjoy!"

"Nice," I said. "So you saw a day—and evening—potential?"

"Yeah. Like, even the wallpaper company could have done more with the space instead of just stacking those long vertical rolls in the window."

"Why not talk to the manager, Ming, and suggest some changes?"

"I wish."

"C'mon, Ming!" Sylvie shouted. "They might pay you or offer to paper your apartment as a trade!"

I encouraged her. "Go for it, Ming. All you need to say is you're a student architect working on a project, and have ideas to help maximize their displays to boost sales?"

"OK. I'll think about it." She smiled shyly and returned to her seat.

"Anyone else hit by some item they want to share?"

Manuel, a young Latino, long black hair covering his face, turned sideways to the class. "Guys, walk east on Seventh Street—before you get to I-35? You'll hit *Koriente*—a Korean tea house - corner of Sabine. The area used to, oh man, it was like, drug alley, right down to the creek. Trash. Needles. Used condoms. Old shopping carts tossed over the side. *Gross!* OK, one day the Korean owners decided … enough! So they planted a little garden in the median strip. Yeah, cute shrubs and rows of wildflowers. What happened? The area kinda cleaned itself up! The diner opposite expanded its deck and came out with a brunch menu. New business moved in. Druggies moved out."

"Because of a *garden?*" shouted a skeptical voice.

"Yeah, man, a friggin' *garden!*" Another voice piped up.

"Manuel has a point, guys," I said, remembering the *Koriente's* great project. "You can change the frequency of a street with a single act." I snapped my fingers. "Clean up a stretch of riverwalk. Add street lights. Renovate the buildings around it as in many other cities. Suddenly those abandoned spaces jump to life. Cafes. Artists' studios."

"Yeah," said Katie, a student with bubbly hair. "Then the locals get priced out."

"Not always," I said. "Not if collectives form around the renovations. Often artists are the first to move in to rehab rat-infested areas. Later, sweat equity can be involved. Anything to avoid gentrification, right?"

"Ms. McBride?"

"Spider?"

"Have the police found the guys who trashed Rory's apartment?"

I froze. All eyes were on me. Spider was a friend of Rory's. I should have guessed someone would throw me back into the moment.

"Not yet." I knew I couldn't get out of this easily. "I'll work through this horror story with Rory." I continued, needing to get off the topic of my nephew, "I've offered my design services to renovate the place. The landlord deserves more than a quick paint job. That space was violated. Brutally."

Spider asked, "How do you restore a violated apartment?"

"You burn sage to cleanse the air," said Sylvie, the young woman in fluffy scarves. "Otherwise disturbed *qi* clutters the space."

There was a groan of despair from the back.

"C'mon, guys," I said. "Sylvie has a point here, no matter how you cut it or describe it. We owe it to a building to transform chaos."

"Call in the exorcist?"

Bursts of laughter.

"You don't need to go that far," I said. "I can step into a house and know immediately if there's discord. Past or current. Sometimes architects are brought in to design a dream house to save a marriage! Trust me. It doesn't work. If I *sense* this is the reason someone wants to commission me, I refer them for counseling."

"Hey, no kidding?" someone asked. "Don't they get mad?"

"Hmmm. Depends on how well we know one another or who referred them. Business contact. Referral from a friend. I always spend time with clients, just talking," I said. "If we don't connect on different levels, there's no point taking the assignment. I give them a list of suitable colleagues."

There was a pause in the room.

Again, Spider spoke up. "Your own property was also violated. How do you transform a murder scene?"

Realizing I hadn't applied my philosophy to my own space, I thought about this for a minute, and then remembered the cascade of butterflies. "Monarch butterflies did it for me, Spider. They followed me as I walked by the bushes and then fluttered around the lantana …"

As I spoke, I thumbed through the shots on my cell phone to find the butterflies. Suddenly I found myself eyeing the earlier shots of Al's head splayed across those same bushes.

My quick flip through the shots added movement to the images and my own sketched update with Rory's help. All of which fused with an awareness I felt as I stared and stared at that head on the baby gurney.

As if on cue, my ears resonated with Sister Colleen's comment, *"Butterflies also followed St. Joan. . . ."* The slow, deliberate way in which she'd said that, exaggerating her Dublin accent with a soft "botter-flies," reminded me of the way my mother would emphasize certain words when she implied something more. It was so subtle, few caught it.

I couldn't believe it had taken me so long to patch the clues together. I lowered my cell phone and glanced up. All eyes were fixed on me. There wasn't a sound in the room. I'd broken my own rule against random cell phone use in class. They knew it. I knew it.

I held up my hands and talked as though on autopilot. "OK. Next assignment? Wander around downtown Austin. Examine ways of avoiding—or maximizing—the Venturi effect in design. Pure physics. Choose a windy day. Plenty of those right now. Oh, and yes," I said, waving my phone in the air. "Shoot some examples on your cell phones or tablets!"

They exited in noisy packs and many of them clustered around me, offering supportive hugs and words of advice.

Spider hung around and said, "Ms. McBride, are you OK?"

"Thanks Spider. Just multitasking."

"These are some of Rory's books," he said, handing me a tote bag. "I borrowed them and promised to return them to his locker. But someone did a smash 'n grab job on it. Maybe the same guys who trashed his apartment?"

I studied the look of concern on the face of this bulky young man in his hooded Longhorns sweatshirt. "Who knows?" I said, taking the bag. "Thanks a bunch, Spider!"

"Hey, anytime." Spider lumbered off, big puffy sneakers squeaking on the floor.

I was glad that a number of evening classes exited the building simultaneously. I wanted to lose myself in the noise. Rory's locker was the least of my concerns.

I called Colleen's cell as I left the building. Voicemail. "Call me immediately," I said. I called Grace and left her a vm. "Grace, I think I know why Rory's being so *damn* evasive."

CHAPTER 19
Wednesday

A vibrant orange mist hung over the lake at sunrise. Typical for this time of year, it reflected the same orange as the monarch butterfly wings. I stood on the hike-and-bike trail and lost myself in it. An observant designer had captivated that similar orange on screens in front of plate-glass windows overlooking the lake in the nearby Four Seasons Hotel.

In the midst of all this horrifying violence and uncertainty, butterflies had taken a gentle route toward me as though to say, *Look at us, watch us, follow us. A otra cosa mariposa,* as the saying went. *Let's move on!* Anyone associated with U.T. Austin was surrounded by that quality of orange, the Longhorn color and trademark that lit up the famous campus tower every time the football team scored a victory. So familiar, so much a part of the Austin landscape!

Before I spoke to Grace, Zuniga, and Isabel, I had to talk to Rory, but I was fed up with leaving messages for him and hearing his excuse about being "out of range or somewhere around the Border without a signal."

So all I did was text him a simple *"I know."*

I kept walking along the path, past a line of bald cypress trees. Their branches sloped downward gracefully, with just a tinge of rust catching the early rays of the sun. I loved the different moods of the lake at this time of the year, loved these clear mornings. I knew as I walked that if

Rory was within range, he would call. I wanted to be surrounded by the lake's comforting beauty when that happened.

My phone chirped in less than twelve minutes.

"Yuh? … ," Rory began.

"I'm not mad at you, Rory. I'm mad as hell at Hugh!"

"I thought you'd figure it out after detective gorilla crossmatched DNA."

"He dropped hints to test me. But withheld the punchline."

"Passing on your left!" A cyclist whistled by, followed by a curly mutt, all floppy and excited.

I waited for Rory but sensed I had to voice it. "I made a mistake about the identity of your half sister didn't I?."

A yellow warbler chose that moment to pierce the air with the most exquisite song in a pecan tree above. Then a mockingbird had to chip in with its own irritating repertoire.

"You're awesome, Buzzy."

"I should have guessed much sooner," I shrugged. "Your avoidance of descriptive details about Al. Sometimes you avoided using pronouns. And the way you blew me off when I thought Teresita was your half sister."

When Rory didn't respond, I told him about my review of the cell phone shots, coupled with Al's resemblance to me in the crumpled color print he found in his chaotic apartment. Then came Sister Colleen's guarded details.

Rory butt in. "OK, Buzz, stop right there. Al dressed as a boy to survive on the streets."

"That's it?"

"Yeah. Transgender? *Nuh-uh.* Not part of Al's street lingo. PC term's *gender fluid*, beyond gender binary. Al liked to talk about being *two-spirit.* As in Indigenous culture."

"Beyond ze, zim, zir?"

"You got it. Or, Al *was* so cool around me. A sister one day and a brother the next. So let's use 'they' to honor two-spirit Al. OK?"

"Sure," I said, regretting that I hadn't been part of Al's life. Rory babbled on about Al's deep rich voice and boyish walk. "So slight they hardly had any boobs. But *wow,* did Al menstruate. All over a towel. Once I had to race out after midnight to grab tampons from a 711 on the Drag."

"So that was the blood the police discovered."

"Guess so."

"How about Al's emotional life?"

"Girls came on to them all the time. But Al's best buddy was a young guy from the same shelters."

I continued to walk along the path, tears coursing down my cheeks.

I crossed over a springy bed of cypress needles to a stone bench overlooking the lake to sit down. Two people rowed by seamlessly, barely rippling the surface of the water.

"Buzz?"

" I'm still here. Hugh tell you anything more about Al's mother?"

"No. He totally shut down when I asked. Said it wasn't a *relationship.* End of story."

I didn't feel like sharing details I learned about Hugh handing an abandoned baby to Sister Colleen, or the details I heard from Penny about Hugh arranging to deport some teenage girl and a baby. Same baby?

"Why didn't your father want me to know?"

"Godammit Buzz. Quit."

"No, Rory. I can't."

"Shit. *Shit!* He said you and Grandma would want to take over Al's life. Adopt. Get Al educated. Organize high school. College.""

"He's right. That's *exactly* what we would have done if he didn't have the *balls* to raise Al." My brother's deceit filled me with disgust.

"Buzzy, Dad said you and Grandma overloaded the guilt trip crap about neglecting me. He couldn't take on another load about Al."

"Is that right?"

"C'mon Buzz. Cut him some slack. Dad was desperate to do right by Al before he died. Like claim fatherhood with DNA tests. Organize retro birth certificates so Al could remain here legally."

"Years after the fact?"

"Don't be so fucking judgmental Buzz. I don't need to hear...."

Static and then the line died. I tried calling back but went straight to voicemail. All I said was, "OK honey. Let's drop it."

Instead, I called Grace.

Once Grace picked up, my words tumbled out. Ducks slid off the rocks below me and paddled downstream.

There was a moment of silence at the other end and then, "Uh, Buzz? Take a few deep breaths. OK. Run that by me again?"

I asked her if Hugh had shared details about fathering Al.

"Al?"

"The kid whose butchered head I discovered."

"What?"

"Come on, Grace. Did Hugh ask you to start sorting out paperwork for a kid he suddenly wanted to acknowledge?"

"Honey, you know how many deranged requests Hugh tossed at me toward the end.?"

"Grace, this wasn't deranged."

I couldn't speak. The ducks came floating back. The orange mist that hovered over the lake earlier had lifted. I gazed across at the dashes of fall colors in the bushes and trees lining the opposite bank of the lake. Jogging figures moved between them like animated pieces of a jigsaw puzzle.

"Buzz, I'm placing you on hold. A client's on the other line. He's boarding a flight and needs to talk."

"Don't blow me off, Grace."

"I won't. I'll call you back."

Rory called again.

"Sorry, Buzz. I lost our connection. What's it going to take you to understand Dad knew Al was in danger once the gangs figured things out?"

"That's why you left Al alone in your apartment?"

"I didn't. Al returned to the Border with me."

"So you saw Al, what, over a week ago?"

"Check. We shared breakfast tacos like I said. Al had dirt on one of the foremen overseeing women in the *maquiladora* Teresita showed you. Sexual harassment. Insisting they logged the minutes they went for pee and/or pooh. Even the pregnant women. Al took cell phone clips and had names they were supposed to give me that evening. But Al never showed up. Never answered my calls or texts."

"Weren't you worried?"

"Buzz, Al was like a hummingbird. Couldn't sit still. Vanishing acts were part of an M.O. No way I or anyone else could control Al's timing."

"Now I wonder why that sounds familiar?"

"Huh?"

I left the bench and started to walk in the opposite direction, crunching my way along pecan shells and granite gravel.

"Rory. It sounds as if Al was murdered soon after you saw them. Someone transported Al's head here as a calling card. You know the name of this *maquiladora* foreman?"

"Could be one of four. Teresita's still digging. Buzz we're both keeping a low profile to avoid endangering guys giving us the lowdown. Sexual harassment's rampant In that *maquiladora.* You complain, you're fired. You gotta believe me."

"I do, Rory. I just wish you'd been open from the get-go."

"Dad said—"

"To hell with that. Didn't you know I'd find out about Al?"

"Yuh, Buzz." Deep sigh. "Can we move on?"

"How does the property deal figure in all of this?"

"It involves one of the *maquiladora* directors overseeing the bully-boy foreman. I can't discuss it."

"Can't or won't?"

Silence.

"Rory?"

"Drop it, Buzz." Rory said. "And don't tell me to get my ass back to Austin."

"What?"

"I'm too busy." Blunt, irritated. Finally, "You and Grace'll just have to work your charm around that hump detective."

He was gone before I could respond. All I could think of was a long hot shower. Then the *Jumping Bean* for fresh fruit, warm, crumbly home-made biscuits, coffee, and the sound of regular breakfast chitchat.

Grace called back as I neared home. I shared the extra details supplied by Rory. She told me to be in her office around noon. "Zuniga'll join us later," she said. "Bring the DVD. Time to throw him a dog biscuit to divert focus away from Rory."

CHAPTER 20

Later, feeling a little more human, I cycled to Grace's law offices in the warehouse district, just a couple of blocks from her apartment. Unlike many lawyers who opted for sprawling antebellum mansions or the cute little wooden houses with porches and shutters like the *Jumping Bean,* Grace wanted the expansiveness of a former Italian restaurant in a redbrick industrial building that—like my own home and studio —was once part of a rail depot. I handled the conversion. We spent time hunting down railway artifacts and huge metal signs from the Santa Fe and Union Pacific freight lines. You walked up steps to a wooden boardwalk and yanked a wrought-iron bar to open the door. Grace's ads and commercials couldn't fail: *"Feeling railroaded? Call Colvin. Vasquez and Li Law Firm at 1-800. . . ."*

The building was opposite parking lots where taco and bratwurst food trucks had been operating for decades. Huge wall art advertisements for local beer provided the backdrop. The adjoining block displayed a classic Austin mix: a vintage movie theater, a world-famous blues club and a high-tech sushi bar.

Grace, son Jerome and their law partners had insisted on a spare, workmanlike interior and I knew her well enough to design just that. The interior still smelt faintly of garlic but that only added a welcoming touch to the bustle.

Bare brick walls sported railway artwork through the decades and African American art from Texas across to the Delta.

Seating from an early Pullman car lined the entrance that doubled as a waiting area. Grace and partners selected music with a Texan connection. Today's choice was Ruthie Foster recorded live at *Antone's.* Clients heard everyone from Selena to Willie Nelson to Janis Joplin, and from Blind Lemon Jefferson to Black Joe Lewis and the Honeybears. Christmas parties usually included a local gospel choir or mariachi band.

"I want anyone from any background to feel comfortable here," Grace had always said. "Sweaty guy straight off a building site. Banker in a Brooks Brothers suit. Latina restaurant owner in a snappy red dress. Black pastor in a cinnamon-striped jacket. Pole dancer in a snaky outfit. *Bring 'em on!"* From the array of folks waiting to see her or one or other of her multilingual partners, that's exactly what she got.

I felt quite comfortable wheeling my bike inside and locking it in a corner of the entrance area.

Grace came sashaying out lip-syncing *"Phenomenal Woman"* along with Ruthie Foster and waved me into her corner office. "Zuniga's running a little late," she crooned, then, eyeing me up and down, said, "Buzzy, can't you dig anything out of your closet except hoodies and painter's pants? Pockets bulging with cell phones and keys? *Shit, oh dear!"*

"Nice to see you too, Grace." I smiled and placed a tote bag on her desk. It held the scuzzy sneakers in a Ziploc bag and the DVD in an envelope. Before sitting down, I helped myself to water from a huge container floating with slices of lemon, lime and orange and sprigs of mint.

Grace grabbed a coffee cup shaped like a squashed face and sat down at her desk in a swivel wooden chair with a leather seat and brass studs—we'd salvaged it out of an old Amtrak ticket office. She leaned over and flipped a switch to lower the music.

"Arrrrright," she said, lifting out the DVD. "Thanks for sending a copy to the office. You have one on file?"

"Of course."

"Don't broadcast that fact, hear what I'm saying?"

"No way."

"Did you persuade Rory to see it?"

"He refused. Point-blank."

"Okay, picking up where we left off by phone," she said, turning to a filing cabinet and removing a blue box folder. "Hugh rambled on in his last month about some kid he'd fathered years ago. All he gave me were these photos." Grace opened the folder, removed an envelope and shook out some baby and toddler shots, fanning them out like a deck of cards on her desk. "You're telling me *this child* is the murdered kid?" She held up a shot of a nun in a habit swinging a laughing baby with black curly hair. I recognized a youthful Sister Colleen.

I nodded. "Can I have copies?" I asked.

"Sure. I 'll scan and email them to you and Zuniga," she said.

"Hugh just gave you baby shots?"

Grace nodded. "Kid was registered as a 'foundling' under the protection of the Church. Hugh wanted DNA tests. But he could never get the kid to go to a lab."

"I think I know why. Al hung around with criminal gangs and had a record—but on the other side of the Border, I heard."

"That shouldn't have been a problem. Doubtful if Mexico has a centralized database. Detectives tell me they wouldn't trust results anyway because of all the corruption in the system. "

I took a deep breath. "Hugh tell you anything about the mother?"

"*Nada. Zilch.* Said she was dead."

"Has Rory seen these?"

Grace shook her head.

Her phone plinked. "Sure. Show him in."

Zuniga appeared in Dockers and a blue shirt so crisply ironed it crackled as he walked in. I rose. After nodding his greetings, "Ms. McBride, Ms. Colvin," Zuniga moved a chair to be able to sit at right angles in the space between Grace and me.

"Detective, this isn't exactly happy families," I began. "I think you knew the victim was my brother's daughter when we met at the medical examiner's. Why dance around the facts?"

Without missing a beat, Zuniga said, "Timing."

"Don't bullshit me, Detective. You were testing me."

"Right, I tried to discover how much you knew."

Swiveling the photos toward him I said, "The baby in those shots is the victim known as Al Sanchez, Al de la Rosa, Al whatever ID was the flavor-of-the-day. Yes, Hugh fathered her and had her raised by nuns. She dressed as a boy to survive the streets and gang life. And described herself as *two-spirit.*"

"Claro," he said, calmly studying the photos. "I suspected there was a McBride connection when I examined Rory's passport at the crime scene," he added, looking at me. "So I had the lab run digital comparisons between Rory's passport photo, your enhanced sketch of the vic, and the crime scene shots of the vic's face. I also placed a rush order on DNA results for confirmation."

I started to say something but Grace held up her hand.

"I'm sorry you had to find out this way, Ms McBride," he added.

I sat back and stared at the ceiling. How was it possible for a stranger to catch something I missed?

"OK, guys, let's move on," said Grace, diplomatically choosing that moment to switch topics. She lifted the envelope with the DVD out of the tote bag and placed it on the desk.

"Detective, this snuff flick has come our way. I warn you. It's one of the worst. It could be connected to more than one murder," she said.

Zuniga held the DVD envelope up between thumb and forefinger. "What's the connection?"

I looked at Grace and she nodded. "I discovered it in Rory's DVD player. I suspect the assholes who smashed up his apartment were looking for this. Not drugs." I added, "I questioned Rory but he denied knowing anything about it."

Zuniga seemed skeptical. "It just grew legs and walked into his DVD player?"

Grace jumped in quickly. "You heard what Rory's neighbor said, detective. Weirdos in and out of his apartment through Halloween weekend."

"Rory was very casual about his keys," I said. "Anyone could have crashed there and left this while he was out of town."

"Still trying to cover up your nephew's irresponsible behavior?" Zuniga asked.

"Detective, my client can't be expected to control her twenty-something pup of a nephew's every step. Or misstep," Grace said.

Zuniga's eyes moved back and forth between us. He placed the DVD on the desk and stared at me. "Ms. McBride? Honesty works both ways here. I'm listening."

Grace said, "Go ahead, Buzz."

"Study the DVD and call me," I said to Zuniga. "I think Al Sanchez's the hazy figure trying to stop the attack."

"Hazy figure?" He asked.

"I can't be sure. But, there's a clear view of the person's sneakers and an unusual zigzag stripe," I explained. "I believe they're the same sneakers I found in Rory's apartment, but they're not my nephew's." I reached for the bagged sneakers and handed them to him. "Your lab can match the sneakers to the clip. If I'm right, the soles might have traces of vegetation or blood spatter from the crime scene."

He took the bag and placed it next to the DVD. "You're pushing it, Ms. McBride. Lifting evidence like this from a crime scene is a serious offense."

Grace rose to her full height and towered over him. "Detective, my client found the DVD *before* the break-in and removed the sneakers *after* you gave the all-clear for her to visit the apartment with her nephew. She's cooperating with your investigation by sharing evidence that may lead to an arrest in more than one murder."

"It's OK, Grace." I butt in.

Grace ignored me. "Detective, your tech experts'll be able to enhance details. Faces, car plates, location." After a pause, she added, "We don't want the DVD and the sneakers hitting the media, social media, gossip blogs and the Hallelujah chorus. … Deal?"

"Deal," he agreed. "DVD's off limits pending investigations."

I closed my eyes visualizing some screaming headline in a supermarket tabloid.

Zuniga replaced the DVD and sneakers in the tote bag, and got up to leave. "I'll touch base ASAP," he said. Then, pausing by the door, he turned toward me and said, *"Comprendo. Lo siento."*

"Si. Gracias. Hasta pronto"

After he left, Grace looked at me quizzically. "What's that all about?"

"Reassuring words sound more meaningful in Spanish?" I shrugged.

"Honey, Eddie's all about tactics. Don't ever drop your guard or lose your cool around Detective Dimples."

"Thanks, Grace."

"Anytime," she said.

We hugged good-bye.

I left Grace's offices feeling even more unsettled and decided to cycle over Ann W. Richards Congress Avenue Bridge to the storage unit where we'd locked away many of Hugh's personal books, research papers and files after his death. I didn't quite know what to look for but was determined to keep on searching for links related to Hugh's time at the Border and the mystery surrounding Al.

I rode by South Congress's funky collection of antiques stores, crafts folk, colorfully painted taco and coffee wagons, a cupcake Airstream, a Cuban cafe, a boutique hotel, a popular cafe with an outdoor space under the oaks for live music and an acupuncture practice in a historic suite of offices once used by an old-fashioned family doctor and a bunch of hookers. All very *SoCo*, as the area was known.

The storage units were off a side street where I hoped to rummage through Hugh's things with a certain amount of privacy. After double-locking my bike within view, I raised the corrugated shutter of his unit, trailing pill beetles, cobwebs and leaves. My lungs tightened. The unit had that typically dank, moldy smell of Austin after an intensely humid summer. U Haul cartons and banana boxes were stacked high, filled to bursting with books, past research files, journals and everything else Hugh wanted to archive at U.T.'s Ransom Center once Rory and I had a chance to sift through it.

I wasn't prepared to hand over Hugh's items cold, like the folks who handed boxes of Isaac Bashevis Singer's papers to the Ransom collection. I had learned more about Singer's life in the assorted junk lifted off his office floor and displayed in a glass cabinet at the library than I could have learned in any biography. Papers, notebooks, tax forms, old letters, photos, chunks of Sheetrock, a slipper and, did I recall, a discarded cereal bowl?

Fortunately I had arranged Hugh's boxes in some sort of chronological order so I knew exactly where to find contents of folders and items dating back to his years on the Border.

I hauled down the largest box and used the tiny Swiss army knife on my key ring to slit the packing tape.

By opening the flaps, I released Hugh's all too familiar smell. Pipe tobacco. And Gauloises. All of which killed him a few months before his forty-second birthday. The dank smell of the storage unit was like nectar by comparison.

I dragged the box outside and took a few gulps of SoCo air. A spider crawled over the edge and staggered away drunkenly. I envied its ability to survive. And to escape. I watched it for a moment and then dug around for archive sleeves where I had tossed bundles of Hugh's letters, along with an assortment of scribbled notes from his pre-electronic days. Hugh left comments, thoughts, eavesdroppings and observations on anything at hand. Old envelopes, menus, road maps, fliers, even in one case, toilet paper. All of which lay in the sleeves jumbled with receipts, crumpled photos and copies of his divorce papers.

I flipped through and placed a bunch of junk to one side to shred later.

My fingers closed over some small hard objects. My father's beautiful ceramic cuff links! I could hardly believe it and remembered searching for them through his personal effects in Panama after his death.

I always loved these cuff links as a child because they matched the deep blue of Dad's eyes. I would get him to place his hands against his cheeks when he wore them so I could call him "Daddy Four Eyes."

It was tempting to sit there and hold them to enjoy gentle memories of Dad many years before we clashed. Instead, fearing nostalgia, I pocketed the cuff links. I continued to shuffle through Hugh's endless shopping lists and reminders and old credit card statements and tax items and crumbling newspaper clippings. All of which he should have cleared and shredded years ago. Or enlisted Rory's and my help in the last year.

After an hour or so, I snapped. I wanted to empty kerosene over everything, light a match and run like hell.

I felt so angry that he had left us all this mess instead of sifting, scanning, and archiving. Long before the cancer spread to his brain, I urged him to get his papers in order. But he constantly brushed me aside. *"For chrissakes, quit worrying, Buzz. Plenty of time to take care of everything. I'm not going to die tomorrow."* Yeah, right.

I kicked the box. Fuck him! *Fuck him!* Why was I digging through crap dumped by TV's great McBride? Smelly boxes crammed with junk? A private life crammed with sleaze?

I kicked the box repeatedly until I my foot got stuck and I had to twist this way and that like a screwdriver to get it out. Files poked through the hole.

I didn't know if I wanted to laugh or cry hysterically.

I yanked out the files and was just about to toss them on the trash pile when a bundle of menus dropped to the floor.

It was the name of the cafe, *Dos Hermanos,* that caught my eye; it was in a small town midway between Del Rio and Fredericksburg.

Hugh's handwriting was all over the menus. Squiggles in the corners implied some sort of sequence.

I raised the menus to my nostrils. Even after all these years they smelled faintly of tortillas. I turned them upside down to decipher the sequence of his vertical and horizontal scribbles between listings for *quesadillas* and *enchiladas.*

Finally, I was able to track his squiggles linking one menu to the next. I doubt if anyone else could have figured it out. I had years of experience with the way he would grab anything if a thought suddenly hit him. It reminded me of the time he wrote the opening paragraphs of a story on a paper tablecloth in an Italian restaurant. A waitperson came by with a fistful of crayons and said, "Sir, would you like technicolor with your salad?"

As I skimmed the menus and found what appeared to be part of an eloquent opening sentence, I decided to dictate the words into my cell phone so it would be easier to fill in the gaps later on. I began:

"Stunning chalk-white cliffs topped by foliage. River a startling blue in the mornings. All you can hear is the endless wind rustling through the surrounding mesquite. I pick my way through thorns and prickly pear cactus. Over rocks pockmarked by rain and fossil trails. Scent of wild oregano is dizzying. River so clear I can count the grains of sand around my toes. Water lap laps against the cliff. Dawn ascent of the sun lifts colors I never imagined out of surrounding limestone and sandstone. Climbed down into the river to wade and swim my way to the hidden cave they told me about miles and miles away from the tourist trail at Fate Bell Cave, I recognize the shaman-like figure who brings the sacred peyote from the heavens."

The next sentences were illegible and covered with smudges and coffee stains. Finally I found one more partial sentence I could decipher: *"I can't believe I shot a girl. . . ."*

I turned the last menu over. That was it. No more words; only a little hand-drawn map showing a curvy river leading into the Rio Grande. Although Hugh didn't label it, I recognized Rio de la Luna.

"I can't believe I shot a girl.." What did Hugh mean? My thoughts jumped to Teresita's comments about Hugh's gun, which Rory was now toting around. I tried to dismiss the thought from my mind. He hadn't said, *"Shot and killed a girl."* I assumed he meant a gun, but maybe he meant a camera shoot? Something related to one of his stories?

That was the last of the menus. I dug around other scribbled notes but could only find some scratchy lists and scribbles on the back of a crumpled American Airlines boarding pass related to one of his stories about blood diamonds.

I replaced the menus in the archive sleeve, intending to scan and enlarge them later, in case I'd missed some fine print or could decipher more of the smudgy words.

Then I came across a bundle of letters tied with string and was shocked to discover they were addressed to Rory.

They were from Penny, his mother. The dates spanned several years of his boyhood and high school years and were unopened. If Hugh had deliberately intercepted them, why keep them? I added them to the sleeve to give to Rory later.

I stared into the interior of the storage unit and visualized the task ahead, but couldn't face doing more right now. I placed the bundle of letters, menus and a few other items in the paniers attached to the back of my bike, along with papers to shred. I resealed the boxes and shoved them back into their prior order.

Just as I shuttered and locked the unit, my phone chirped.

It was Sister Colleen. I began to wheel my bike into the road.

"Are you on a landline?" I asked, unwilling once again to risk the poor quality of trying to communicate with her cell to cell.

"I am indeed," she said.

"I know about Al," I said simply.

"Ah. I knew it wouldn't take you long. I dropped enough hints, did I not?"

"Mom was Irish. It's not hard for me to catch your subtext."

"I begged Hugh to talk to you and your parents about Al."

"What was his excuse?"

"He said it was too complicated."

"Too complicated for *him* you mean. Wouldn't have been complicated for us." I continued walking along with my bike.

"I can't hear you so well, Buzz," she said.

"Sorry, I'll go up a side street." I turned off Congress onto Elizabeth, to a more residential area.

"We could talk later?" she suggested.

"No way. You're too hard to reach."

"I made inquiries about the land as you asked."

"And?"

"You were right. Passed to the Diocese some years ago. Rented out for grazing purposes mainly. They tell me it's beautiful. So beautiful there's gossip about one of those fancy-spa companies buying up parcels of the best land overlooking a curve of the river. Planning some extravagant retreat with a safari theme and rock art murals. It's all about rich tycoons paying *thousands* for cactus wraps and to have their toes tickled to try and lose their flab isn't it?"

Her voice dripped with sarcasm. My hackles rose. Some kids started to kick a ball around their front garden so I continued to walk my bike to a quieter spot under the trees farther along.

As Colleen spoke, I recalled Hugh's eloquent words about the area, scribbled on the menus. I then remembered references Rory made to some "Mickey Mouse resort deal" involving "laundered money". Was this it?

"Colleen, did your sources mention the name of this safari-spa outfit?" I asked in between her comments about "pampered slags" spending more on a "spa weekend" than her "annual budget."

"Ah … Crossroads? Crossovers? No, wait. *Crossing Lines.* Something like that."

"Crossing Lines?"

"I believe that's what they said. Trying to honey up to the Diocese with the word 'cross'? Oh spare me." After a pause, she said, "I've to go now, Buzzy, Running late. Let's text if we find ourselves phone-tagging. Bye. God bless."

I said good-bye and sat on my bike staring at the trees separating the neat row of single-story houses ahead. Then I called Carlos, and asked him to scout around any safari-themed spa proposal named *Crossing Lines* that might—officially or unofficially—involve any feasibility studies on Diocesan "parcels" of Rio de la Luna property near the Border, not far from Del Rio.

CHAPTER 21

Wednesday, later.

Dusk was falling rapidly these days. A time when trees and lights reflected themselves in the dappled waters of Lady Bird Lake. At night when the wind was still, the air felt quite velvety. The lake turned all shades of dark metal. Fall colors tinged the trees bordering the trails. Soft yellows, dusty pink, rust and an occasional dash of red. A time of year I usually relished, with long balmy days after the intense humidity of summer. At this moment I didn't have the heart to linger and appreciate the extended fall. Everything I did felt like triage, prompting Rambo-style hits on Hugh's storage unit and Rory's apartment. It wasn't in my nature to run roughshod over family privacy, but what choice did I have?

I cycled away at top speed, retracing my route to the lake, and wove my way between hikers and dogs along the trail. My head bulged at the thought of the internet digging I still had to do.

Normally I would cycle home around unfamiliar streets. Nothing I loved more than an abandoned or vacant building to quicken my senses as I visualized a creative adaptive reuse. Or a way of inspiring my students to visit specific sites for projects.

Instead, I decided to head straight to my studio, because I was beginning to feel badly about overloading poor Carlos. Horis and Doris met me on the trail and trotted behind me, I'd been neglecting them too!

"Hey, Buzz. you look like you been dumpster diving," he said as I walked in with the two cats at my heels.

"Close," I smiled. "I think I earned one of your cappuccinos."

"You got it," he said. "Hey Kitties!"

Carlos cut a tall, stately figure. His thick, black braid hung down his back like an exclamation mark.

After graduate school, he'd interned with me, and that made him indispensable. His skills were sharp. He danced around all the newest CAD programs with ease and efficiency, plus he was great with clients.

Unlike many freshly batched architects, he could also use a pencil *and* enjoyed building models. He shared my design philosophy and funky practice and took care of mundane details like ensuring we paid our bills on time. Oh, and did I mention he was a former *Jumping Bean* barista and made great cappuccinos? We snapped up their old espresso machine when the owners upgraded a few years ago.

Our practice spread across the entire upper floor of the former rail depot. Huge plate-glass windows on two sides and skylights offered wonderful natural light and panoramic views of the hike-and-bike trails all the way down to the lake and rowing club. With a combo of solar panels on the roof and rain-harvesting gutters and tanks and the high percentage of local and recycled materials used in the rehab, the depot was a model of green building design.

If we couldn't provide a living, breathing showcase, how could we persuade clients to aim for LEED certification? The lower floor housed a carpenter/sculptor we often commissioned to design and install Texas wood floors and cabinets for our range of projects.

Carlos walked over to the espresso machine and brought me up to speed, reassuring me that everything was moving ahead and it was OK for me to continue to take a few extra days. "Go for it Buzz," he emphasized. "And the kitties are fine. Look!" He nodded as they jumped onto the window seat.

I knew this. But apart from never ever wanting to take advantage of him, I also yearned to return to the order of my professional life.

Being in this lovely space under the skylights, with comfortable seating surrounded by photographs of our best designs, made me sense how fragmented I had become.

It took me a moment to realize Carlos was telling me about the internet search he had made, including some discreet calls to contacts to find out which possible spa organization had been sniffing around the Border.

"Someone came up with a name that sounded like Compass," he said, whooshing the foam and swirling a little heart shape on top of my cappuccino. "No website or anything. Just some business execs trying to cash in on the spa craze. My contact thought *Crossing Lines* was a working title for one of the schemes."

"Any links to some existing organization? Hotel chain?"

"Still digging. No clue on investors but the cash offer to the Diocese was huge according to loose talk around a couple corporate water coolers. Oh, some hot-shot banker commissioned a feasibility study of possible sites in the area."

"No direct mention of Rio de la Luna?" I asked, reaching for my cup.

Carlos shook his head. "Just West Texas, not far from Amistad Dam. Everything's broad and vague," he said, fanning out both hands.

"My nephew hinted at a Border deal involving money laundering. My other source mentioned a possible safari-themed spa for pampered tycoons."

"Hmmm, could be," said Carlos, busily preparing an espresso for himself.

"Compass," I mused, and thought immediately of the long vertical lines crisscrossed by shorter horizontal lines on the pink binder on Rory's desk. Well, not exactly symmetrical, but close, and a possible logo for either Compass or *Crossing Lines.*

Shaman-like or *compass-like?* Or something in between? Either way it was a simple logo that could cut both ways.

I took my cup over to the computer and tried to ignore the pile of papers loading my in-tray. I google-mapped Rio de La Luna and zoomed in. I gazed at a series of overhead views. Hugh's scribbled words rang in my inner ear.

Yes, glorious chalk-white cliffs. Crystal waters gushing over rocks. I visualized hikers and kayakers and tubers enjoying the refreshing feeling of that spring-fed river to cool the senses during the peak of summer. If the area had just been used mainly for grazing, it probably looked exactly as Hugh described several years ago. I did some skillful matching of details I recalled of his map on the menu to try to pinpoint the exact curve of the river he described and the possible site of some hidden cave off the tourist trail.

Carlos looked over my shoulder. He sipped his espresso thoughtfully. "But why that spot? What's so special about Rio de la Luna?"

"Incredible beauty. Spring-fed river in a drought-ridden area. Unexplored rock-art in hidden caves."

"Come on, Buzz. Factor in the expense of building roads, power and sewage lines."

"Millions."

Carlos exhaled. "Cartels are laundering their money through deals like horse-training ranches and restaurants, like the recent raids right here in Austin. No one's going to see their money going down the tubes on *la frontera* in a spa. Unless," he said, raising his cup. "Unless the land has hidden reserves we don't know about. Oil? Natural gas?"

I thought about this for a moment, remembering the *Be Careful Where You Drill* signs as I entered Del Rio, alerting folks about as yet untapped areas of natural gas. But I shook my head. "Nuh-uh. Too simple. Too Texan."

Carlos rolled his eyes. "Buzzy, Go home and rest."

I followed his advice, wheeled my bike home with the cats, and offloaded Hugh's papers from the paniers into boxes. But rest was impossible. Carlos had offered a reality check and I began to wonder whether the so-called safari-themed-spa ideas were diversionary tactics.

I had left Carlos with the task of rattling his contacts for more details, including digging around to find out if anyone had ordered an aerial search for any possible hidden reserves as he suggested.

Discoveries of natural gas and the highly controversial fracking methods to release those lucrative reserves were currently hot topics in the state.

The thought of oil and gas drilling and roads for huge tankers destroying that pristine Rio de la Luna beauty was nauseating. Or, was the spa planned far away from the drilling for oil executive types for conferences and playtime? If cartel money laundering had been exposed in horse ranching and restaurants in Austin, it would make sense if new ventures involved remote areas of the Border. Would a safari-themed spa be the sort of venture Rory could sniff out faster than gas drilling?

I also wondered about the intentions of this alleged spa and possible exploitation of sacred symbols or hunting themes dating back thousands of years in the rock art caves along that area of the Border.

I opened my laptop on the mesquite bar and pulled up references to the rock art of the lower Pecos River. To orient myself, I accessed the Fate Bell Shelter, which I'd visited some years ago in the Seminole Canyon; it was about forty miles west of Del Rio on Highway 90.

Certainly there was nothing online, in the current tourist information or on a Texas Parks and Wildlife site, about the Rio de la Luna cave Hugh referenced in his scribbles on those *Dos Hermanos* menus.

It was highly unlikely that any Luna cave—accessible only via the river—was generally known, except perhaps to archaeologists, who continued their research and documentation of the cave art of the lower Pecos. Even most Texans were unaware of those treasures in remote spots along that slice of the Border. Rock art caves on private land were often inaccessible and off limits, to avoid trespassing and vandalism. Not every cave site was protected.

I was sensitive to the mysteries of the hunter-gatherers who created the rock art, which dated back some four thousand years. Their shaman-like journeys were embedded in the narrative of the art. Mythology and symbolism revolved around hunting, to honor the sacred animals and plants necessary for survival and especially during migration.

Once again, I thought back to the day Hugh, Penny and I visited the Fate Bell Shelter and how dismissive Hugh was of our varying interpretations.

Or, on reflection, was he feigning indifference and ridicule because he had something to hide in that area?

As I revisited the rock art online, how well I recalled a feeling of awe, standing there gazing up at the pictographs, and especially at that triad of anthropomorphic figures—including the winged, antlered anthropomorph symbolizing, perhaps, shamanic journeys into the beyond. The artist in me responded to the symbolism associated with the sacred deer, believed to bring the first peyote cactus with its hallucinogenic and medicinal uses, thought to grow in the deers' hoofprints. Equally sacred was the datura plant.

The use of plant and animal dyes on the cave walls ensured the figures would share their stories and messages for generations through several thousand years. Nothing was casual or transitory about this art.

Similarly the budding architect in me studied the layout of the cave shelter, the middens (the remains of the cooking areas) and how dwellers organized their sleeping and bathroom needs, with little regard for privacy. Well, privacy by our modern standards, not by theirs.

I could remember feeling a need to whisper as I stood there; I'd been increasingly irritated by the tourists surrounding us with their dumb questions and oohs and aahs, as well as their noisy cameras in those pre-digital days. Not to mention those whiny kids who wore flimsy shoes that hurt their feet on the sharp rocks, and their stupid father who asked the guide, "Did these graffiti artists cross the Border illegally?"

One thing occurred to me. If the Diocese was in the process of selling—or had sold a parcel of land—it wasn't in a position to object to any future business venture involving sacred rock art in a cave that honored a shaman-like journey the Church would consider "pagan" and full of "idol worship"? Unless, in the cunning and exploitative spirit of the early Spanish missions in the area, they could somehow justify the sale by implying the imagery and symbolism was "transformed" by "Christian" overtones, in the way they had supplanted many Toltec and Aztec rituals. I could just imagine some priest at the Border warbling on about the image of "the Ascending Christ" in an uplifted rock art figure, implying a state of visionary ecstasy.

Hence the possible Catholic acceptability of the logo of long vertical lines crisscrossed by short horizontal lines, on the binder I'd noticed on Rory's desk. The name *Crossing Lines* was apt. At a distance, that recurring geometric form was at the core of the many variations of anthropomorphs, but, equally comfortable for the Diocese perhaps?

A cunning way of sanitizing a deal involving laundered money?

Hugh would have been quick to spot that. How did all of the above reflect on that historic deed the Ortiz family had been obliged to pass on to the Diocese? Or did that conveniently end, giving the Diocese *carte blanche?*

Either way I was determined to find out. I added yet more lines to the items on my whiteboard. I also sketched a line of anthropomorphic figures to anchor myself in history.

Because of his own heritage, Carlos knew a lot more about the symbolism of the rock art than I did, so I called him at home. He was busily reading a story to his five-year-old twins and promised to call me back. Which he did, within the hour.

"Twins asleep?"

"Yeah, right. They're having a pillow fight. Hey, as long as it exhausts them, we're cool." He chuckled. "What's buzzin' the Buzz right now? More spa deals crossing *la frontera?*"

"It's that hint about the rock art murals," I said, filling him in.

Carlos was quiet for a few minutes. I could hear TV in the background.

"Honey, I'm going in the kitchen," he called out to his wife, Connie.

"Say hi to Buzz," I heard her yell back. "Invite her for dinner. All I ever see of her is a hoodie cycling away from reporters on TV."

"Say hi and thanks to Connie," I smiled.

"OK," Carlos began. "You know how I feel about business morons messing around with our symbols?"

"Carlos. I don't know anything for sure. I'm working on hunches."

Carlos sighed. "How does Rory figure in all this?"

"That's the problem, Carlos. He's Mr. Evasive."

"Sure he isn't just getting stoned with a bunch of dudes? He's a student,

Buzz. They try everything. I did at his age. Didn't you? Hallucinogenics out in the Chihuahuan desert? Creating fantasies out of the shooting stars?"

"No," I said.

"No, as in you know for sure he isn't? Or no, as in you never indulged?"

"Hey, I indulged! But I don't think Rory's out there tripping." An image of a drunk Rory hanging in the doorway in Acuña suddenly jumped into my mind. How could I be sure of anything? "Carlos, I'm so sorry," I said suddenly. "Taking up your family time and doubling your workload at the office. This isn't fair. I'll drop in tomorrow morning for a couple hours. I need some sanity."

"Buzzy, don't overload. Listen, I'm clocking up free time when all this blows over. Thinking of taking Connie and the twins to Port Aransas during Thanksgiving week."

"Plan on it, Carlos."

After we said good night, I decided to take the plunge and try Isabel once again, implying more than I actually knew. A classic tactic used by trial lawyers.

I called her cell phone, left an urgent vm, and also texted her and sent an email. All I said was *"Discovered Hugh's secret. Call me anytime 24/7."*

She returned my call shortly before midnight.

After the call, I listened to a Celtic trio, and drifted off to sleep. My dreams were full of glimpses of Hugh chasing Rory through animated rock art images of hunting scenes.

CHAPTER 22
early Thursday

Dawn began to stab darkness with red streaks. I forced myself awake. After grinding beans for coffee, I went to steam my senses under a long hot shower before doing some serious Tai Chi to work stiffness and exhaustion out of my body. Horis and Doris nestled in my duvet and watched every move.

I burned sage from my garden, not only to cleanse the air but to clear my thoughts to be able to return to work in a few hours, before driving to meet Isabel.

The night before, once I'd greeted her with the words "Hey, Agent Isabel," there was silence on the phone.

Then: "Buzz that's the past. I quit Border Patrol years ago. Too heart-breaking. I couldn't stand picking up families cheated by *coyotes* and left to die or stumble around crazed in that heat. It was the kids that got to me."

"Do you ever really quit Border Patrol?"

"You didn't call to talk about that. If you want to discuss Hugh, I can see you tomorrow in Kerrville after my lunch meeting. "

"Can we talk now?"

"No way. Not by phone."

Isabel's tone was short. Clipped. Businesslike.

Kerrville was a convenient meeting place roughly midway for both of us, neither her turf nor mine. I got the feeling this might be my only chance to meet her face-to-face to resolve some immediate issues unless I drove all the way to Del Rio.

Something I couldn't handle right now.

I fixed myself a mango, banana and yogurt smoothie for breakfast. Today I couldn't face rattling over to the *Jumping Bean* for a "regular" breakfast and chatter. I took the hint about my clothes from Grace, Carlos and Connie. It made me realize I hadn't even had a chance to do anything as basic as laundry. Last time anyone used the machine was Rory, and it didn't occur to him to toss in some of my clothes.

I dug jeans and a polo shirt out of my closet and opted for a swirly aquamarine jacket to uplift my mood. When I walked over to my studio, a delicious smell of wood wafted through the open windows of the carpenter/sculptor's workshop on our first floor. I paused, drawn by the pitch of a power saw in a shaft of sawdust. Normally such sights and sounds were an everyday part of my life and I didn't take a second glance. Today they gave me hope.

Carlos was out. I studied the calendar and saw he had an appointment with the planning commission. I checked our progress list on the whiteboard. Terrific! Carlos had someone lined up to renovate Rory's apartment, with completion confirmed by Thanksgiving. He left a couple of queries next to a renovation of a jazz club and cafe under way in east Austin, and the planned adaptive reuse of an automotive body shop into a martial-arts studio in north Austin. Oh and yet another request for one of our famous *catios!*

I was just about to tackle these when my phone chirped.

Zuniga.

I might have guessed an escape into my own safe world was to be short-lived.

"Ms. McBride, we're still harvesting info from the DVD. License plates suggest Texan *and* Mexican Border towns. So location could be either side of the Border. If it's Mexico, we pass everything to the relevant authorities." After a pause, he continued, "But you were both right—and wrong—in your assumptions about the shoes."

"Shoes?"

"Those sneakers you found in your nephew's apartment."

"Oh, right. Sure."

"Our forensic photographer was able to match the sneakers *exactly* to the individual's sneakers and logo in the DVD because—as you noted—there was a clearer shot of the sneakers and soles than of the individual wearing them. Well-worn shoes carry specific marks, signs of age, foot shape and so on."

"Great work. So my assumptions were right. What did I get wrong?"

Zuniga paused. "The guy in the sneakers was not Al Sanchez."

Stunned, I asked, "How can you be so sure?"

"Our lab experts do great work with body dimensions. The sneaker guy is now a key witness."

"So we're back to square one?"

"No way. Lab is enhancing the faces to cross-match them through face recognition info from CCTV camera footage on the Drag and around campus near your nephew's apartment. In case the same gang in the DVD totaled your nephew's apartment."

There was silence on the phone.

"Ms. McBride, your nephew could help us track down sneaker guy. There's a clear match between fingerprints on the sneakers and prints we lifted from your nephew's apartment. The guy could still be in Austin."

"Detective, I can't even be sure my nephew *knows* the guy. You heard what his neighbor said about weirdos in and out of Rory's place at Halloween."

"Uh, Ms. McBride? How closely did you study that DVD?"

"I tried to block the rape and mutilation," I admitted.

"I thought so."

"Why?"

"As I mentioned, Al Sanchez wasn't trying to stop the attack. Al Sanchez *was* the victim."

I sat motionless after Zuniga's call. A total shock? Not really. I had a sinking feeling when I flipped through photos on my cell phone during Tuesday night's class. Then I began dancing around with doubts. I was too cowardly to attempt to view the DVD again. I had to pass that task to the detective.

Brushing my teeth barely got rid of the acid taste in my mouth so I reached into a desk drawer for a stash of chewing gum. Finding it impossible to block the memory of the savage clips in the DVD, I scribbled a message to Carlos on the whiteboard, and left. im

I used my jeep to meet Isabel in Kerrville. To hell with rental cars and camouflage. At this point I was beyond desperate to find answers and resolutions.

I recalled the haziness of the faces in the DVD. Would it even be possible to track the rapist/killers through face-recognition technology? Through matches in the database? By circulating images around law enforcement in the state? Or by good old fashioned police work involving street snitches? But if the perps were over the Border? Gangs? *Maquiladora* bully boys? I didn't think we had a chance in hell of finding them.

I toyed with the idea of discussing the DVD with Isabel. I didn't intend blowing her cover if I discovered she was still connected to Border Patrol.

I had to wonder if she lent me her vehicle to track my movements on both sides of the Border. It was so easy for her to swap keys, even though she wasn't on my rental agreement. She was far too savvy, and too hard to reach, just to be a cafe owner specializing in *tamales.* The location of her business on Highway 90 was an excellent listening and observation post for traffic crossing the Rio Grande. Maybe those two Border Patrol agents I saw leaving her cafe were more than just customers?

I decided to be diplomatic when I met her. I'd play the anxious sister card, trying to find out more details about a dead brother.

In Kerrville, I parked close to a cafe in Knapp Park overlooking the Guadalupe river where we had arranged to meet. Since I was early, I chose a table in the window with a view of the river and ordered green tea.

To distract my thoughts, I tried to guess which of the waterbirds lifting off the river had once skimmed by me on Lady Bird Lake. A laughing gull soared overhead, probably on its way up from the Gulf.

Isabel appeared forty minutes later, a very different Isabel from the flamboyant cafe owner. Her hair was tied back and she wore a demure charcoal gray suit and white stock blouse. A striking woman in any outfit. It wasn't hard to recall the photo of her in a Border Patrol uniform in Hugh's story. She looked as fit and as athletic today as she did then. But with no time for chitchat or small talk, that was very clear.

"Why don't you tell me what you know, Buzz. I'll try to fill in the blanks," she said, after sitting down and ordering black coffee.

I then told her what I had discovered about Hugh fathering a daughter during some escapade with a teenage girl. "I heard your father was also in Border Patrol then and—allegedly—had the girl and baby deported."

Isabel didn't react.

I fast-forwarded to recent events and my dig through Hugh's clips.

She was silent for a few minutes as a waitperson poured her coffee. Then, circling the cup with both hands, she looked at me and said, "Hugh made mistakes."

"Don't spare me, Isabel. I'm losing all illusions about him. There had to be a good reason why he quit the Border after breaking the Ortiz cousins' drug smuggling and murder story. Where did the teenager and baby fit in?"

Isabel glanced around the cafe and said, "let's take this outside." She signaled to the waitperson for the check and some to-go cups and sugar.

We replenished our hot drinks, left by a side door and down a grassy slope toward the river's edge. Avoiding a noisy group of geese, we aimed for a picnic table under a sprawling cypress tree.

"OK," Isabel sighed. "This is a toughie."

"Nothing could be worse than what I've heard to date."

She went on. "Del Rio was very proud of its cultural heritage and the contribution of famous ranching families—especially those Spanish families under Don Ortiz. Until the town was shaken by the family's murder scandal."

"I understand."

"I don't know if you do, Buzz. It's about an old Spanish sheep-ranching family everyone knew. They owned land dating back to the days when the Spanish king handed out chunks of Spanish territories to noblemen, priests, *rancheros,* as favors. Or to expand the missions."

I nodded and told her I had googled the Ortiz story and legends.

Shaking a little packet of sugar into her coffee, Isabel said. "After the Alamo, some families lost land in Texas. Grabs, or illegal purchases. Or," she went on making no attempt to hide her disgust, "Some *hijos de putas chingadas* in the Texas Rangers helped Anglo ranchers seize land owned by Spanish families."

"So it was quite unique for a family like Ortiz to to retain valuable ranching land on both sides of the Border?" I asked.

"You bet. Over the decades, unwanted chunks were sold or ranched by cousins, nephews. But—the jewel in the crown—was that Rio de la Luna land. The most fertile and beautiful. They vacationed there. Had wedding pictures taken next to the spring. As high schoolers we were invited for special cookouts and camping weekends or swimming parties. The land was sacred."

"So losing it was...."

"Devastating," she butt in, adding, "That's where one story ends and another begins. With Hugh and the family Ortiz."

"You mean his story about the renegade branch of the Ortiz family? The grandma drug connection?"

Isabel studied my expression.

"What?" I asked.

"Oh Buzz," she sighed. "You're so innocent. You see the best in people. Don't you?"

"I try to."

"Hugh wasn't just a journalist," she went on. "He knew about the Ortiz tradition. For the oldest son of the oldest Ortiz son to inherit that Rio de la Luna land, he had to be born on the Mexican side. Even if the family mainly ranched and lived in the U.S. Daughters didn't count."

"Course not."

"When your brother was at the Border, he was buddy buddy with the oldest son, Jesse Felipe. Some say he was in love with your brother."

"Ah, so Jesse Felipe tipped off Hugh about the drug connection?"

"It wasn't that simple."

"Isabel. I know how Hugh played people." I couldn't bring myself to ask if Hugh's report on the drug smuggling resulted in Jesse Felipe's murder.

"Jesse Felipe was stunning," Isabel began. "Champion gymnast with the soul of a poet. Eyes like melted chocolate and the body of a Greek god. I was at high school with him. Sure, he tipped off Hugh about his cousins' drug-smuggling operation," she nodded.

"I thought tight families like that never disclosed the darker sides—especially to a gringo like Hugh?" I butt in.

"It's a long time ago, Buzz. But still painful. Couple of years after his marriage, Jesse confided in Hugh when he discovered he was sterile. Complications after a bad case of mumps as a young teen apparently. Humiliation? Macho guy from that historic Spanish landowning family? The next Don Ortiz everyone adored and looked up to? Jesse Felipe knew his scumbag cousins were running the grandma operation—just one part of a drug- and human-smuggling cartel. He couldn't stand the decline in the family."

I took a deep breath. A young couple ran by tossing a frisbee in the air for a Labrador.

"You really want to hear this?" Isabel asked.

"I don't have the luxury of choice."

Isabel dropped her voice and told me how Jesse Felipe became desperate to father a son to protect the family inheritance and restore the good Ortiz name. He was the only son in a family of girls. Huge responsibility. Otherwise that rich Rio de la Luna land would pass to the Diocese, according to the original Spanish deed. To honor the mission established by Padre Pablo Ortiz. "Jesse expressed such passion about that land," she went on, "his words sound as beautiful in English as in Spanish."

"Can you quote something?" I asked.

"I can only summarize a few haunting lines. Something like. … '*I move through thorns and prickly pear cactus. Over rocks pockmarked by rain and fossil trails. I walk in the footsteps of my ancestors intoxicated by the scent of wild oregano. . . .*'"

My memory pinged. I lifted up my cell phone and played the clip

I'd recorded of words on the menus I discovered. *"All you can hear is the endless wind rustling through the surrounding mesquite. . . ."*

Isabel looked at me in amazement. "You found Jesse's poems?"

I turned off my cell phone. "Not exactly. I came across words Hugh scribbled on a cafe menu. I should have realized they sounded too poetic to be his. He must have deleted the references to ancestors when he lifted Jesse Felipe's text."

Isabel's eyes filled with tears and she looked away.

I knew where this was going. "Let me guess," I said. "Beyond the poetry, Jesse Felipe asked Hugh to . . ."

"Oblige? More than that. He knew Hugh had a taste for unusual sexual flings. It wasn't difficult for him to ask Hugh to impregnate Rosa, his young wife, with all three of them in bed together, night after night. He was in love with Hugh. So the request came with a bonus."

"Rosa went along with this?"

"I doubt if Rosa was even consulted. She came from an indigenous family."

Isabel paused. "She was just a teenager and very beautiful. I believe Jesse Felipe really loved her. He refused to marry the daughter of another landowning family - against his father's wishes. Jesse Felipe and Rosa were certainly outsiders."

Which made the relationship with Hugh all the more plausible. "So Hugh's narcissism flourished ?" I asked. "*And* he got the story about the drug smuggling as a payoff?"

"You got it."

"Wow," I said.

"Soon as Rosa's pregnancy was confirmed, Hugh got exclusive scoops on the smuggling story, connections, routes, names of corrupt officials and politicians, including a well-known senator. Didn't you know that's how he got his break into TV?"

I didn't because I was studying abroad at that time. Also those reports were absent from his clippings and digitized articles.

"But the hyped-up tripod of Hugh, Jesse Felipe and Rosa resulted in a daughter? Not a son, right?" I asked.

Isabel nodded. "Bitter irony?"

"I shot a girl"—Hugh's comment on the menus I discovered in his storage unit—now made sense. Neither gunshot nor photo shoot. Just ejaculation.

How dumb could I be not to figure that out? I sat back and stared up at the clouds streaking across the sky. Now I understood how the Ortiz jewel of Rio de la Luna passed to the Diocese, and why Hugh quit the Border.

I also understood the source of one of Al's names, de la Rosa.

"What happened next?" I asked.

"Jesse Felipe's cousins Pepe and Adolfo tortured the truth out of him. They knew about his problem. They sliced off his *cojones* and stuffed them in his mouth," she said, fluttering her fingertips in front of her lips. "Then they shot him, execution style, up against a wall, and slowly. First his knees." She looked down. "I found his body."

Neither of us could speak for a moment.

"I had nightmares for years," Isabel admitted.

"God Almighty," I said. "Were the cousins ever arrested?"

Isabel shook her head. "*Bastardos cabrones cogidos.* They vanished into the interior of Mexico. Pepe was killed in a drive-by shooting by some rival cartel hitman a few years ago in Mexico City. Piece of shit. His ending was too quick."

"And Adolfo?"

"Still in business. Involved with a minor cartel."

"What happened to Rosa?"

"They claimed she died in childbirth and the baby didn't survive. Later I heard they paid some *doula* to let her bleed to death. Rosa's terrified teenage sister, Lupe, managed to escape with the baby girl and ran to Hugh for help."

"So *that's* who my sister-in-law, Penny, met at their front door. Your Dad had Lupe deported?"

"For her own safety. I know Hugh took the baby to a convent. We then told him to get the hell away from the Border ASAP. Before he died, he tried to make amends. It's OK Buzz. Rory's filled in the blanks. About Al."

I rose and walked to the water's edge where the huge cypress tree was partially rooted. In that moment I couldn't stand the frivolity of the couple tossing the frisbee close by.

"What happened to Jesse Felipe's parents and sisters?" I asked finally.

"His parents were broken. One of the sisters—Gloria - made it her life's work to take care of them until they died. The others? They married and moved as far away from the Border as they could."

"Do they keep in touch with you?"

"No."

I stared at the river and said nothing.

Isabel whispered, "Buzz we don't need to talk about this anymore. Except.....knowing what I do about the family ... I suspect Adolfo Ortiz paid his dogs to behead Al and trash Rory's apartment to prove his power over the McBrides."

I wasn't so sure. "Why wait all these years? Why not just track down Hugh and kill him like they killed Jesse Felipe?" I couldn't believe a creep like Adolfo would waste time on us within a year of Hugh's death. It didn't make sense.

"At the Border - sense doesn't make sense," said Isabel. "C'mon. Let's go!"

We crumpled our cups and tossed them in the nearest bin, and ran up the grassy bank towards our vehicles parked in the road. I hugged her for a long time and watched her drive away. I sat in my jeep without moving and just stared at the river. Then I began dictating every detail I could recall into my cell phone, before heading back to Austin.

CHAPTER 23

Later on Thursday

I was so lost in thought on the road home it took a few moments to realize a call was coming through. It was Sister Colleen.

"Buzz, are you somewhere private?"

"I'm in my car."

"It's urgent."

"What's up?"

"Strictly confidential. No police. No lawyers. Am I clear?"

"I give my word."

"Short time ago, I got a desperate collect call from Joaquin."

"Who?"

"Joaquin? He knew Al in our shelters. He's barely sixteen and on the run. Holed up in an abandoned house in north Austin. Rundberg area I think he said? Near I-35 and North Lamar Boulevard? I'm on the road right now to find him. I need your help. You know Austin well. I don't."

My heart skipped a beat. Why she would call me and not one of her religious contacts? We figured out how long each of us would take to meet. I gave her an easy address to locate outside a well lit gas station and convenience store on North Lamar.

Joaquin? The name didn't ring any bells, though Colleen spoke as though I should know who he was.

As I had plenty of time before meeting her, I drove home first to change into dark jeans, hoodie and sneakers, not just to match my mood, but to blend with the night.

The Rundberg area in north Austin had a troubled record. Its shifting ethnic mix—Middle Eastern, Asian, African American, Latino and Anglo—was marred by an undercurrent of neglect, poverty and unemployment. The tiny portion of Rundberg's population involved in petty crime and drug dealing cast a shadow over a neighborhood that included gated communities flanked by wooded and green spaces. By contrast, seedy motels provided magnets for drug deals and sex trafficking close to I-35, a heavily traveled corridor extending from the Border to the main central cities of San Antonio, Austin and Dallas, and northward up through the Midwest.

Unfairly perhaps, "Rundberg" was associated with shootouts, domestic violence, bodies found in dumpsters and drug deals.

As I drove there, I sensed that recent grants involving the police, U.T. Austin's sociology department, and local community groups for environmental changes, could not come soon enough. "Broken window" policies would oblige neglectful landlords to tackle repairs as a way of reducing crime. Master gardeners were directing volunteers to help xeriscape grounds at key schools in the area. The intention went way beyond beautification.

Some blocks like those I took as shortcuts desperately needed resurfacing. Dim, flickering streetlights cried out for upgrades. Transforming two-way to one-way streets would certainly reduce traffic and make it harder for drug dealers to race back and forth.

I'd introduce the concept of Crime Prevention through Environmental Design, nicknamed *CPTED,* in my next class for the student architects.

Until then, I realized that someone on the run probably felt safer in such a mixed, poorly lit neighborhood, where his accent and body language would not be instantly recognized or rouse suspicion. He would be one tiny flutter in the shifting shadows.

Because it was turning into a cold windy night, I picked up a few containers of hot chocolate and some burritos to share, and waited for

Colleen in the parking lot of the gas station's convenience store as arranged. I kept an eye out for her old truck. Instead, a battered, dark blue Toyota whined up beside me. Turquoise rosaries, carnival beads and feathers dangled from the rearview mirror. Colleen took one look at my yellow jeep, rolled down her window and said, "We'll use my car, Buzz."

I swung my legs out of the jeep, locked up, slid in beside Colleen and handed her one of the hot chocolates. "Grand," she said, downing it in seconds.

"OK, Colleen. Rundberg runs east and west off North Lamar. Did he mention the Y on west Rundberg as a landmark? It's like a beacon."

She shook her head. "I believe he said head east a few blocks toward I-35. Turn left at a *taqueira.* He's in a broken-down place opposite some two-story apartments. I couldn't catch the name of the street. Oh, with an old truck in front propped up on cinder blocks. Not far from North Lamar."

"Oh baby," I groaned. "'Not far could mean anything. Let's get cracking. Head left here and left again at the lights."

The old Toyota shuddered out of the parking lot. Several twists and turns later we were bouncing our way up a very dark block. She filled me in quickly about Joaquin. "Both Al and Joaquin grew up in our shelters and drifted into the same gangs, Buzz. I don't know how he got to Austin. He's terrified. Says gang members tried to kill him near campus."

Apparently Joaquin walked miles up North Lamar to an address someone in Del Rio gave him. But the place was abandoned.

After about ten minutes, I told Colleen to do a U turn and retrace our steps. I thought I had spotted a truck up on blocks between two buildings but wasn't sure.

"He said it would be in front," said Colleen.

It turned out to be an old discarded postal van covered with spray paint and gang turf graffiti.

The place opposite was in total darkness.

I could just make out a broken roof and sagging front porch. A rusted doorless fridge lay in a pile of garbage.

I recognized the style of housing from decades ago. It had probably been someone's pride and joy before poverty or the family's deportation sealed its fate.

Colleen rolled down her window, placed two fingers in her mouth and gave three short, sharp, very unconventlike whistles.

Frantic yapping came from one of the apartments. A guy with braided gold hair and tattooed biceps opened a window and yelled, "Fuck off!"

"Trust me to wake up the neighborhood," said Colleen.

"He probably thinks we're trying to muscle in on his crack turf," I said. "We may need to circle the block again."

Colleen placed a warning hand on my arm and nodded to her left. A slim, slight figure in a hoodie belted out of the shack. She stretched over the seat, and opened the back door. He slid in without a word. "You're safe, *mi'jito,*" she said softly. Gears grinding, she shot away from the curb.

"Hungry?" I said, passing food over my shoulder.

Shivering, he grabbed the bag without a word and began to devour the burritos and tear the lid off the hot chocolate.

He ducked in a quick shaft of light from a passing car, but I caught a brief glimpse of his hooded, dirt-streaked and terrified face. With a shock, I thought I recognized him.

"Where now?" said Colleen.

"Keep going to the end of the block and turn left," I said.

My senses told me Joaquin needed a shower and a change of clothes. If he was on the run, and my hunch about his identity was right, the only solution was to take them both to my place, before Colleen headed back to the Border.

"Oh, no need, I don't want to trouble you," she said.

"Come on, Colleen. You can't risk police pulling you over in this rattletrap. They'll take one look at Joaquin and suspect you're harboring an undocumented kid. You don't want them descending on your sanctuary."

We zigzagged our way back to the convenience store to pick up my jeep.

Joaquin had eaten the entire bag of burritos and downed two containers of hot chocolate before we pulled into the parking lot.

Unclipping my seat belt, I said, "Just follow me. Do you have GPS on your cell phone?"

"Don't be ridiculous," she said. "It's a dinosaur."

"OK, I'll be a second," I jumped out, unlocked my jeep, scribbled my address on a scratch pad with a simple map in case she lost me en route.

"At this hour of night it won't take us long," I said, handing her the map. "Best to avoid the major highways. It's a straight shot south on North Lamar to downtown. Watch the descending numbers on cross streets and turn left on Fifth. I'm two minutes from there. Any problems, call me."

I glanced over my shoulder. Joaquin lay curled up in the fetal position on the backseat, head buried in his arms.

"The lad's OK," said Colleen. "Probably the first time he's slept in days. Can we go? I need a loo and a good cup of tea,"

She sounded like my mother. I swung onto North Lamar. The Toyota shuddered after me, engine whining.

I kept Colleen in my rearview mirror, reducing speed whenever I lost her at the lights on our way south.

When we neared downtown I motioned to her to keep in the left lane. She called as we turned onto Fifth Street.

"Buzz? We have to stop."

"We're two minutes away."

"Problems. I'm pulling in here."

I glanced in my side mirror. She drove into a parking lot in front of a gym. I stopped behind her.

"Joaquin's panicking, Buzz. He can't stand light. "

"OK, follow me down this side street. My studio's in a darker area. Away from the apartment complexes. Take a sharp right at the end and keep going until you see a two-story warehouse."

I heard her exchange some muffled words. Then, "OK," she said.

Moments later she parked beside me. I unlocked my studio and deactivated the alarm.

Head down, the boy streaked out of the Toyota and into the building. I pointed out two rest-rooms, one with a shower, at the top of the stairs.

I had installed this shower to use after site visits in summer months. I dug out a red flannel shirt, gray fleece sweats and socks for Joaquin from an assortment in the closet.

Colleen emerged from one of the rest-rooms. We could hear the shower going full blast in the other. Steam began escaping under the door.

"These'll be a bit loose on him," I said, handing her the clothes and a large bag for his discards.

"Oh, lovely. I'll drop them outside the door for him. Now then. Can I put the kettle on?"

"No," I said, walking over to the espresso machine. "This is the best way to get blistering hot water. What would you like? Ceylon? Assam? China? Green? Or Earl Grey? Rooibos?"

"Jesus, Mary and Joseph," she said, glancing around. "No shortage of creature comforts! I'll take the strongest in the house. Long drive ahead."

I hit the button for boiling water, swilled warm water around a teapot, emptied it and reached for a tin of Assam tea.

"You could rest on those couches," I suggested, nodding at our comfortable seating around a table laden with architectural magazines.

"Ah no. You're most kind," she said, glancing at her watch. "We'll leave in a little while. Best to cross the Border as soon as possible."

"What about those Border Patrol spot checks before you hit the bridge?" I asked.

"I'll be wearing my veil," she winked, sweeping a hand over her auburn curls.

Joaquin emerged from the shower, pink and scrubbed, enveloped in the gray sweats.

He paused and lowered his head

I dimmed the lights. "Spanish or English?"

"His English is good, Buzz. I taught him."

"I figured. Here, Joaquin!" I tossed him a can of soda. He caught it with both hands and popped the lid. I reached into our small fridge for milk and prepared a tray with mugs, sugar and teapot. "How about some soup?" I suggested.

'Whatever takes the least amount of time and trouble," she said. "Joaquin?"

"Cool."

This was the first time I heard him speak. I opened a couple of tins of corn-and-fire-roasted-veggy soup and emptied them into a pot on the hot plate.

Moments later I ladled it into three bowls, shook a bag of multigrain tortilla chips into a dish carved out of a log, and we carried everything over to the conference table. Colleen poured tea for us both, a comforting and familiar sound.

Joaquin ate slowly this time, and kept peeking at me as he reached across the table for tortilla chips. He had delicate features, with large brown eyes and thick, glossy black hair, damp from the shower. It took a stretch of the imagination to recall the violence he had witnessed, including days on the run in an unfamiliar city.

I looked at him and said, "Joaquin, I know how you fought to save Al."

He moved his empty bowl to one side, crossed his arms on the table and put his head down. Colleen reached over and placed a hand on his shoulder. She glanced at me with the expression of someone who was beyond shock or surprise.

I wasn't about to tell her about the DVD and how I thought I recognized him from the brief glimpse in the car earlier.

I guessed he wasn't afraid of lights but was afraid to go near my home because he had been there before. My hunch was confirmed when the night Amtrak train screeched to a halt at the station nearby. Colleen jumped but Joaquin glanced in the direction of the noise and gave the hint of a smile. I sensed he had probably jumped the rails from Del Rio to Austin.

I also knew I had to remain calm, though I felt anything but inside, realizing I had put this kid in danger by handing his sneakers to Zuniga. The detective described him as "the guy" he had to track down and question about the gang rape and murder of Al.

They now had Joaquin's DNA, fingerprints, sneakers and his description. I wondered if CCTV cameras caught his image on the Drag?

If apprehended, he could wind up in juvenile detention. If forced to name names, he faced a grisly death in juvvie. Because I was stupid enough to hand his sneakers to Zuniga.

I tried to dismiss fear by saying, "Only someone who loved Al would take such a risk." I added, "Bringing Al's head to my tree so I would find out about the murder?" I didn't say that I believed he tried to cover Al's face with a white mask out of respect.

Joaquin straightened and stared at me.

"You are courageous and honorable, *si, muy fuerte y honorable,*" I said.

Colleen withdrew her hand. "Joaquin, what happened *mi'jo?*"

"They want to kill me like they killed Al," he said, making a chopping motion across his neck.

Colleen said. "I'm taking you over the Border to a safe house with a *curandera.* We'll work something out," she added, glancing at me.

"Joaquin," I said, wishing I felt as reassuring as I sounded. "Who are *they?* Who paid *them* to butcher Al?"

He swallowed hard.

I reached over and gently pushed up the sleeve of his sweatshirt after I noticed him pull it down over his hand. A tiny wing and curved beak was tattooed between his first and second fingers.

"Aguila?" I asked, remembering the fragment of a feathered tattoo we had noticed on the hand of one of the attackers in the DVD.

I looked at the nun and the gang member. Their silence was confirming. A gang was using the eagle symbol? Familiar symbol of both Mexico and the USA? I should have guessed that of a Border gang.

Joaquin placed one hand gently over the tattoo.

After a moment, Colleen said, "Give Joaquin a chance to cut loose. Don't ask him to be a snitch, Buzz. Too dangerous. You don't understand."

"Oh, I understand, Colleen. We all know what happens to a snitch."

"He has to protect himself by disappearing, Buzz. Don't push this. *Please!*"

I turned to him. "Joaquin, you knew Al was my niece, *mi sobrina,*"

He nodded and gazed sadly out of the windows.

"Two questions," I said. "Why didn't they kill you when you fought the attack? And how did you escape with Al's head?"

Joaquin opened his lower lip to show me his eagle tattoo. He began talking slowly in a Border mix of Spanish and English, explaining the ritual required of him to earn his gang "acceptance" tattoo.

They made him bring Al to them late one night in Acuña for "discussions" about a "stash house" they planned in Austin for *maquiladora* workers they said could find jobs with a cleaning service. They knew Al had "connections" in Austin.

"I believed them," he said.

Colleen closed her eyes and took a deep breath.

Tears began to roll down his cheeks as he described, quietly, how they drove Al and him in the back of a pick-up over a bumpy dirt road to an open area, where they joined a circle of vehicles and a bunch of guys he didn't know.

When they saw the fire pit and beer coolers, he and Al thought they were going to party. Everyone got wildly drunk and high. He made gestures to show they were snorting and popping pills provided by a guy he suspected was a *sicario,* a cartel hitman. Then the guy started to strike Al and tear off her clothes. Someone produced a machete. Joaquin covered his face.

"It's OK Joaquin," I whispered, recalling the DVD. "No need for details."

He began to speak in broken sentences, enough to tell me the other guys were so wasted after the attack, they didn't notice him placing Al's head in one of the smaller coolers.

He was given the task of collecting the empty bottles and dumping the garbage when they returned to the Border. He then grabbed the cooler and ran.

"Who were the 'other guys'" I asked. "Were they also *Aguilas?*"

He shrugged and said he heard they worked for one of the *maquiladoras.*

"Did they say why they killed Al?" I asked.

"Many reasons. Someone paid them. Al talked a lot. Made threats."

"Threats? Can you tell us more?"

"No."

Colleen said, "Joaquin? Al deserves dignity *mi'jo.* Help Al's young soul find light."

He glanced at me and said, "I tried."

"You jumped a train to Austin then went to my nephew's place, right?"

Joaquin nodded and said, "The guys discovered where I was hiding. They smashed up your nephew's apartment when they couldn't find me and the D...."

"It's OK, Joaquin. I found it," I butt in, unwilling to raise the topic of the DVD in front of Colleen. I went on, "Question. Who paid them to kill Al and..."

"That's enough," said Colleen. "Buzz, this is dangerous. The *sicario* can ID Joaquin."

"Trust me, Colleen. Joaquin, where did they kill Al?"

He glanced at the ceiling. It was after midnight, he explained. They drove through a very rocky *colonia,* up a slight hill. Bad, bad road. He and Al nearly fell out of the back of the pickup. They circled at top speed around bits of a truck sticking out of the dirt.

There couldn't be two trucks like that I thought, remembering my drive with Teresita. "You passed the truck on your right?"

"Si."

"Roughly how far did you go after you circled the truck bits?"

He said he couldn't remember how long it took but they drove until the road ended. He made a T sign with his hands. "No houses. *Nada.* Some cacti. A few trees and bushes. Very rocky. And then the fire pit in a hollow," he said, forming a bowl with his hands.

I made a mental note of everything he was saying and went to my computer to google the area and print out snapshot aerial maps. "Keep talking," I said, wary of breaking the flow. "Did they just dunp the rest of Al's body there?"

He nodded.

Colleen rose. "Buzz we've to go," she said. "Joaquin, help me clear up." She took the dishes to the sink and began running hot water.

"I'm driving to the Border with you," I said.

"Buzz, don't be insane. There won't be much of that poor child left. You don't know what it's like. Coyotes. Vultures. I've seen what happens to the carcass of road kill. Joaquin? We've to go. *Now.*"

Sensing her panic, I packed fruit, sodas and the rest of the tortilla chips in a tote bag and handed it to her. I also reached into a cookie jar kitty and stuffed several twenty-dollar bills into my back pocket.

Joaquin began to unzip the hoodie and reach into the bag for his dirty clothes as if to change back into them.

"Hey," I said. "No way. Sweats are yours to keep. And I have something else for you."

Colleen clattered downstairs, but he paused, bag in hand.

I reached into my desk drawer for a spare iPod and earbuds and handed them to him with a pack of chewing gum. I also grabbed one of my old Longhorn baseball caps and placed it backward on his head. "Wear this. Chew gum. Hold your head high if police or Border Patrol stop you. OK? If you want to survive, you need to act cool. *Si me entiendes?*"

"Si."

I showed him how to access music—everything from rap to Mexican ballads to hiphop.

"Joaquin," I said. "You did everything you could to save Al. Don't forget that. The *curandera* will help you get through this. Get a tattoo artist to transform your eagle symbols into something else—anything. OK?"

He kept his head down and nodded once.

"Buzz?" Colleen called from the bottom of the stairs.

"Coming!"

"I need you to point me in the right direction."

"I meant what I said, Colleen. I'm going with you."

"Sounds grand but the answer is no"

"The answer is yes. Soon as we cross the Border we're going to that fire pit."

"We most certainly are not."

"We most certainly are."

Joaquin turned to me and said, "When Sister Colleen talks like that, you can't argue with her."

"We Irish love to argue," I smiled. "Ignore us."

Joaquin mumbled something under his breath about being surrounded by women with *cojones.* He followed me downstairs, waited for me to lock up and set the alarm, and then hesitated before walking to the Toyota.

"Miss Buzz?" he said softly, nodding in the direction of my home. "That pecan tree where I placed Al's head? … It was … *muy importante."*

"Por que?"

"Al used to sit there. To watch you. It gave peace to Al. Al two sprits."

I fought back tears, unable to speak for several seconds. "Al told you that?"

"Si."

Everything I had learned about Al in the last few days found a tenderness in Joaquin's few words. Joaquin, on the run, a former gang member traumatized by the murder of a beloved buddy, starving and filthy a couple of hours ago, now standing before me fed, showered, wearing my Longhorn cap and gray sweats.

"You want to ride in the jeep with me?" I asked him.

"*Si.* But best I go with Sister Colleen. Keep her talking and singing so she doesn't fall asleep at the wheel."

"Oh, of course."

He climbed in beside Colleen and didn't look back. I walked to the driver's side as she finished a call on her cell phone.

I ignored her exasperated expression and suggested the easiest route out of town.

"I always knew you McBrides were 'touched,'" she said, tapping the side of her head. She tossed a black veil over her curls "Don't go speeding and lose me now."

I jumped into my jeep. As a precaution I quickly texted Rory to let him know I was on my way to the Border. Then I fired up the engine and swung toward Fifth Street. The old Toyota rattled into the darkness behind me.

CHAPTER 24

Thursday-into-Friday

We stopped once midway for gas and coffee, to stretch our legs and take a potty break.

Colleen did everything in her power to persuade me to turn back. "No common sense. *None* whatsoever," she said when we emerged from adjoining stalls in the rest-room.

"At least I'm not boring," I smiled.

"Exactly what do you plan to do once we cross over the bridge?" she asked, as we pumped soap onto our hands and rinsed them in unison.

"You know what I'm going to do. With or without your help. Let's keep going. I want to get there before dawn."

We dried our hands and returned to our vehicles in silence.

Joaquin was fast asleep, head resting on the back of his seat, my Longhorn cap pulled down over his eyes.

Colleen sighed and reached for her keys. "Buzzy, when we're through saving the living and the dead," she said, "we'll sit together over a dish of tea far from here. Dublin perhaps?"

"There's a thought." I said, jumping into my jeep.

A sixteen-wheeler thundered by in the night. A truck pulling a huge trailer came clattering behind.

We waited until the taillights vanished before we swung back on the road. I knew it would be impossible to relax until I saw the Welcome/*Bienvenidos* sign for Del Rio with its friendly sun-and-wavy-river logo, and passed by Garcia Gas and other familiar landmarks my headlights illuminated in the dark. It would be impossible to relax until I felt sure we wouldn't be stopped anywhere on the road for any reason.

As the stickers on Colleen's window enabled her to cross the bridge faster than I might, she called and suggested I continue on after I crossed and gave me directions to a yellow slab of a store named *Casa del Duce* where she would wait for me.

I held my breath as I drove through the historic district toward the bridge and aimed for what I hoped to be the fastest lane, until I saw the large banner *Bienvenidos a Ciudad Acuña, Coahuila,* over the entry point. If I thought it would be less busy to cross in the dark I was quite wrong. Huge delivery trucks slowed the way ahead and I lost sight of Colleen.

I was so focused on inching along without rear-ending the guy in front, it took a moment before I realized someone was tapping on my window. I caught a glimpse of a short, burly figure in a black leather jacket.

I assumed it was someone trying to catch a ride over the bridge and ignored him. The tapping turned into a clenched fist thumping my window. I heard someone shout, "Ms. McBride!"

Bulky shoulders. Baby face. Stunned, I lowered the window and said, "Jezuz *Chrrrrrrist!*"

"No. Eddie Zuniga. Open the passenger door," he said, and sprinted around my jeep before I could respond. Moments later he jumped in beside me.

I couldn't believe this. "Of course it's just a coincidence you happen to be walking across the bridge at 4.57 a.m., right?"

"I parked my car when I saw you." He gave a dimpled grin.

"Aren't you out of your jurisdiction here?" I asked.

"Who said I was on duty?" As we continued to inch forward, he pulled adhesive off a sticker and pressed it to my front window. "This should speed things along," he added.

I tried calling Colleen, but bounced into voicemail. There was no way I could turn back. I pleaded with her in my thoughts to get Joaquin safely through the Border and into the shadows before she saw me.

Trying to sound casual, I asked, "Did you attach a GPS tracking gadget to my jeep this week?"

"You have a creative imagination."

"So the answer must be yes."

"The answer is no."

My hackles rose. I didn't respond. We inched toward the entry point.

There were fewer army vehicles around compared with my previous visit. When a uniform approached from a brightly lit office, Zuniga lowered the window, showed him his ID, and spoke rapidly in Spanish. The guy just waved us through without a second glance.

"Keep going," Zuniga said.

There was no sign of Colleen's Toyota ahead but I recognized the familiar whine over the noise of the traffic. I glanced in my rearview mirror. She emerged out of a side street, two cars behind me. A moment later, the passenger door opened and Joaquin darted into a well-lit *pasteleria* filled with workmen.

I saw the sign for *Casa del Duce* ahead and pulled over.

Colleen parked behind me, got out, casually walked toward us and said, "Hi, Detective Zuniga."

I opened my door and said, "*Excuse* me?"

She winked. Without missing a beat, she explained, "I called him before we left Austin when I knew what you intended to do."

I looked at Zuniga in amazement. "Is this true?"

He nodded and said, "I was an hour away. No big deal."

I felt like an idiot. Though relieved she had taken the precaution of offloading Joaquin in advance, I couldn't help saying, "Since when do I need a guard of honor?"

"Since right now," she replied. "Detective?"

"We'll go to the fire pit in this," he said, slapping the side of my jeep. "The Toyota can't handle those dirt roads. No offense, Sister."

"No offense taken."

"Hello?" I said. "Do I have a choice here?"

"No," Colleen said. "Saddle up."

I knew it would be over an hour before dawn began to hurl gray streaks at the darkness like an artist tossing paint at a wall. Streetlights flickered like fireflies and then died. Cars, pickup trucks and huge delivery vehicles lumbered by us from the bridge.

Zuniga reached into his leather jacket, removed his police revolver from a shoulder holster and checked the safety catch. "*Sta bien?* Let's go!"

Colleen climbed in the backseat. "OK, Buzz. I know the shortcuts to the *colonias.* Keep going and turn left at the next junction. Then first right."

After a pause, she added, "In case you're wondering Buzz, I told the detective I got an anonymous tip-off about the killing fields. I made the mistake of sharing this with you." She fixed her gaze on me in the rear-view mirror. "I should have known how you'd react."

"Un-huh?" I said, returning the stare.

I followed her directions. It was cool to be all heroic and in control in Austin. But I had to concede. We were on her turf now. Not mine.

I took a sidelong glance at Zuniga in his black leather jacket. "You look like a hood."

"Great. I hope everyone else thinks so," he smiled.

"You never let go, do you, Eddie, 24/7?"

"Do you ever stop buzzing?"

""Shut up the pair of you! Take a sharp right by that container shack," Colleen butt in.

We bounced over stones and jumped a pothole. We passed a dip and I recognized the privy Teresita had shown me days earlier. Five people were waiting outside. I now had a sense of the route we were taking. A line of workers walked by us.

"The night shift," said Colleen. "Keep going."

Recalling my maps, I had a rough idea of mileage and with luck we would hit the fire pit within ten minutes, depending on road conditions. As I drove, I remembered Cecilia Balli's words in that *Texas Monthly* article about the condition of butchered body parts left scattered in the desert. I also knew there was nothing Zuniga could do except pass information through to his Mexican counterparts, because the murder had occurred in the state of Coahuila, not in Texas. I asked him when Sister Colleen and I could dignify Al's remains with a decent burial.

"After we file our final forensic reports" he added. "If Sister Colleen's informant is correct about the murder location."

I caught her gaze in the rearview mirror. I knew how protective she was of Joaquin but she had no idea the crime lab in Austin had his sneakers and DNA thanks to my stupidity. I had to hope the said "informant" remained anonymous.

I swerved to avoid hitting something large and black that darted in front of the jeep and loped along the side of road, wings flapping.

"It's a buzzard. We're close," said Zuniga. "How about slowing down?"

We were in the stark and rocky terrain Joaquin described beyond the *colonia.* My headlights picked up piles of rocks, a few leafless trees and some clumps of prickly pear cactus on both sides of the road.

I spotted a dip ahead. "Maybe we should park here and leave the lights on before the road ends," I suggested.

"Touch nothing," Zuniga warned as we climbed out.

I took photos of my tires and tire tracks as a precaution when or even if local authorities processed the alleged crime scene and picked them out over the scores of tire and truck tracks that crisscrossed the end of this dirt road.

The wind changed direction. We all clamped our hands over our mouths.

"I don't know if I can go through with this," I said.

"Oh blessed St Jude," Colleen groaned. "Tell me Buzz is not thinking about bailing on us now, will you?"

"Huh," I responded, quickly placing my fingertips and thumbs together to create close-up frames to see if I could match landmarks from the DVD.

Zuniga held up his cell phone with clips from the actual DVD and scanned the area to pinpoint angles.

"Down there," he said, pointing at blackened stones in a fire pit. The wind scuffed old embers and bits of blue cloth. Something pink seemed to be impaled on a cactus. My memory produced a quick snapshot of Al's macheted and bloodied body in that exact spot. The elements and animal scavengers had reduced her to scraps.

Colleen made the sign of the cross and waited quietly at the edge, head bowed.

I began taking photographs in an arc, needing panoramic views to distance myself from the indignity of it all.

I was the first to speak. "Look at that strange tree over there." I pointed, walking toward it. "The wind's strong enough to twist its shape."

"Buzz, stop right there," Zuniga said quietly. "That's part of a leg stuck between the branches."

CHAPTER 25

Early Early Friday

I drove recklessly all the way back to downtown Acuña. The jeep's springs were tough enough to take it, but Zuniga and Colleen held onto their seats and pressed their feet into the floor as though we were about to launch into space. If either of them told me to slow down, I didn't hear it. As we neared the *Casa del Duce,* I did a U turn, ignored the chorus of angry hoots and screeching of brakes and parked on the opposite side of the street, close to Colleen's car.

Colleen climbed out and her legs buckled. She held onto the car door handle and said, "As the late, great poet Seamus Heaney said, T*he kite takes off, itself alone, a windfall.* Buzz, none of this is new to us. It's new for you. Grow up. Call before you leave the Border?"

"I will."

"Detective, we're depending on you."

"I know, Sister. We appreciate your help," he said, reaching out to clasp her hand between both of his.

"Keep an eye on that impossible McBride," she added over her shoulder, digging in a pocket for her car keys.

I noticed the way she glanced in the direction of the *pasteleria,* where I hoped Joaquin was still waiting for her. As I swung my jeep around, I told Zuniga I wouldn't achieve any sense of peace until those bits of Al had been removed and examined by local authorities.

"Buzz, they might not all belong to Al."

"Oh God. If they can't be identified I hope we can bury everyone together. At least?"

"I'll see what we can do. I know one of the homicide detectives here. I'll brief him within the hour. You need to talk?"

"Maybe," I said, turning left. "There's a quiet tree-lined plaza a few blocks from here."

"Go for it."

I remembered the route from my previous visit. Folks were crossing the plaza on their way to work There was a smell of coffee in the air but it nauseated me, so I kept the windows shut. I parked opposite the fountain and placed my head on the steering wheel. Zuniga sat in silence beside me.

After a few moments, I lifted my head and said, "Check the foremen in the *maquiladora* closest to the *colonia* we just passed," I gave him the name of the manicured site Teresita had shown me. It was a long shot but I remembered what Rory said about Al 's sniffing around for dirt on a foreman's bullying and sexual harassment tactics. If what Joaquin told us was right, I had to assume they butchered Al to keep Al quiet and to make money by posting the snuff flick on sites creeps paid to download.

"I'll pass that along," he said.

"Unless the guys are in the wind by now. Any hits on the vehicles' plates in the DVD?"

"All stolen. One set belonged to an eighty year old retired teacher from Laredo. Someone lifted them and attached them to a stolen vehicle. The faces of those kids in the DVD have hit every law enforcement and Border Patrol computer. "

"Meanwhile Al's murder DVD's probably gone viral by now," I said, hoping Colleen was driving Joaquin as far away from here as possible. I didn't dare ask if the CCTV cameras on the Drag matched any faces from the DVD.

Zuniga didn't respond.

"Detective?" I asked.

"We used the DVD as bait."

"*Bait?* I thought we'd agreed..."

"It's OK ," He explained. "Our tech guys in vice tracked it on a snuff site they've been monitoring. Downloaders lit up across the globe. We tracked several local viewers we're keeping in our sights. And we were able to close down the site."

"Unless it's doing the rounds of some sicko voyeur club." I said, thankful at least that Al's face was partially hidden. "Can't your tech experts track whatever video equipment was used? IPO? Maybe an iPhone? Everything leaves a fingerprint."

"Claro," Zuniga agreed. "We don't have such high tech resources. Now that we can locate the alleged killing fields, I'll talk to the FBI."

Again, I prayed Joaquin would never bounce onto their radar.

"Even if we track the killers," Zuniga continued, "We know they are way down the cartel food chain. We suspect this isn't just gang violence. The Border comes closer every month. Hits on judges. Money laundering through horse ranching and restaurants in Austin. Our intel told us one minor cartel boss planned to use your brother's funeral to mask a little activity."

"Let me guess. Was the boss Adolfo Ortiz? My brother pissed him off years ago. So that's why you were staked outside the Cathedral?"

"Something like that."

"False alarm? Or a warning?" I asked, remembering what Isabel had said about seeing the hand of Ortiz in any hit on my family. I didn't believe her at the time.

He didn't respond. A text bounced into my phone. I ignored it.

Zuniga glanced up at the chalk white sky and at his watch. "*Basta.* Buzz all we can do is keep chipping away at cartel control," he said. "I'll touch base with you and Sister Colleen ASAP."

Before he climbed out, I said, "Detective, I know you're pushing boundaries here. You've pushed boundaries your entire life, right?"

He gave his dimpled smile and pulled up his sleeve to show me the remnants of a tattoo on a bicep. "Gang life at twelve. Kung fu coach at the Y pulled a bunch of us off the streets and shaped us."

"I might have guessed. A few nights ago you quoted your mother. How did she handle your gang life?"

"She died before I hit the street. She was undocumented. From Mindo, Ecuador."

"I know Mindo. Stunning rain forest. And what fragrances! Those huge sunflower bushes overlooking the river are scented like honey."

Zuniga looked at me in amazement. "You know *Mindo?*"

"My father's engineering work took us all over South America."

Zuniga sighed. "We'll talk about Mindo another time. *Hasta pronto,* Buzz," he said, jumping out.

I sat and watched him walk briskly across the plaza, cell phone at his ear.

A second text chirped. *"RU close? At Emporium on Main."* I texted back. *"On my way."*

I tried to ignore the smell of bacon, clatter of plates, and laughter and made a quick dive into the *Emporium* restroom.

Rory and Teresita were huddled together ordering blueberry pancakes at the counter. He was wearing one of Hugh's suede shirts and designer jeans.

Rory swung off the bar stool and opened his arms to me as I approached.

"I'm beat," I said. "This isn't a social call. Hi, Teresita!"

"Heyyyyy." She smiled warmly. "Mom tells me she had quite a visit with you."

"She should write her story," I said.

"That's what we keep telling her. What can we order for you, Buzz?

"Bottled water."

My voice sounded clipped but I was done with a soft approach. "Rory, can we move to a table? We need some privacy."

Teresita took one look at my expression and said, "You guys go ahead. I'll wait here. No problem."

Rory said, "Babe, you don't have to sit apart from us! Come on, what is this?"

She placed one hand on his shoulder. "Rory, Buzz needs time alone with you. It's important." She smiled at me and reached for her cell phone.

"Oh *man!*" he said impatiently, gesturing to the waitperson to bring his pancakes and coffee to the table—with bottled water.

Very briefly, I told him I'd driven through the night for the sole purpose of examining the pit where Al was killed.

He stared at me and said, "You got to be fucking kidding me. With a cop and a nun? And who else? George Lopez and the Comedy Channel?"

"That would have helped." I nodded.

He shook his head. "Buzz, why can't you move on?"

"I am moving on Rory, OK? Quick questions. Quick answers?"

"I told you I'm not returning to Austin," he said.

"That wasn't one of my questions."

He shrugged.

I took a chance and jumped in. "I believe you know some outfit plans to move laundered money into a fancy spa and deer park called *Crossing Lines at Rio de la Luna.*"

Rory lifted his fork. "C'mon Buzz. You're not that naive. Laundered money going into a spa and deer park? Seriously?" He popped a large chunk of pancake into his mouth.

"But I heard—"

"Forget it," he said between mouthfuls. "OK, maybe a spa's included for jacuzzi and rubdowns after a day of hard hunting. Exotic deer are also involved."

"Hard hunting?"

"Get real. We're talking one luxurious game reserve to outdo Escobar's private reserve! They're planning to fly in exotic animals from illegal networks in Southeast Asia and Africa. List is stunning. Bengal tigers, onyx, lemurs," he said, reaching for his coffee. "Don't forget rhinos, wildebeest and springbok from South Africa. And some kangaroos from Australia for fun. Hey! Smuggling exotic animals ranks after drugs and weapons!"

"God *almighty.* So rich businessmen can play safari games and shoot animals paraded for the kill?" I realized "safari" wasn't just a "theme."

"Long hunts. Quick canned hunts. Trophy kills," Rory itemized. "Each package costs a fortune. Depends on the endangered species some guy wants to decapitate and skin for his wall at home. Oh, and global live-streaming to an exclusive club of guys happy to pay *thousands* to watch slow kills. Ground is being broken as we talk. Including a landing strip for executive flights and private helicopters."

I couldn't believe what I was hearing. Live kills beamed around the globe? How far would that go? Same sickos who watched teenagers like Al raped and butchered?

What next? Interactive games?

I had driven by other private game reserves in Texas, with their tall security fences and armed guards at the gates. Acreage was so vast no mortal could peek inside. All perfectly legal, including fancy paperwork to mask the origins of the animals. CBS's *60 Minutes* reported on the owners of such exclusive game farms, who felt they should be congratulated for their "conservation programs".

I sat back while Rory finished his stack. Rock art images of hunting scenes ribboned through my mind. So the owners planned huge murals of those images to paceset and stimulate rich businessmen's hunter-gatherer fantasies?

"You mean the Diocese *agreed* to the deal?" I asked Rory.

"Oh, Buzz, hello? You know how the Church is offloading property to pay those multimillion dollar lawsuits! They're not in a position to pick&choose buyers!"

"So?"

"Dad found out about this and started to dig around but got too sick to complete so he involved me. Sleazy dude called Ortiz made an offer ...."

I couldn't believe this. "*Adolfo* Ortiz?" I asked.

"Dunno. They call him *Aguila*."

"Oh JesusGod." I said. "So his gang butchered Al?" Events of the past few days began spinning in my mind. *Aguila*/Ortiz? *Aguila*/Gang? And Zuniga leaning against the huge bronze Eagle outside the Rusk building after my brother's funeral? Coincidence? Or, to warn Ortiz there were bigger eagles out there watching him if he considered using my brother's funeral for some action?

Rory paused as a waitperson refilled his cup. He turned toward Teresita. "Babe, I need your help here?"

Teresita rose, twisted her long tresses over one shoulder and glanced at me to make sure it was OK before she joined us.

"Guys," I said. "Did you know Al's birth mother was married to an Ortiz linked to that land? Years before any of this *Aguila* shit?"

"Oh, Buzzy, who cares? Al was supposed to inherit money from Dad but Dad died before it could be finalized. Al went ballistic and started to throw threats around."

So that explained the angry calls Al had made from Ruben Flores's phone and money transfer prefab center I visited in Del Rio.

Rory babbled on, "I tried to help Al. But things got messy. Al was on a fast track to disaster. Buzz, not even your best intentions..." He looked at Teresita, and went on, "Ortiz discovered who Al was. Some asshole started a rumor that Al planned gender reassignment surgery to claim to be the rightful male heir to the Ortiz land. All total bullshit, believe me. Al enjoyed duality. But I doubt Ortiz even knows the meaning of terms like *two spirit.*"

Teresita added. "it was the *maquiladora* foreman who started the rumors to ingratiate himself to Ortiz. And to silence Al. We had Al in there under cover to help us unionize the workers. Huge mistake. We screwed up. I'm sorry Buzz. I'm very, very sorry. And the foreman has vanished of course."

"Sorry isn't enough," I said. "I'm not blaming you, Teresita. I blame Hugh."

The three of us sat in silence.

"Buzz, don't go pissy on us. *Listen* to me," Rory insisted. "Dad knew Ortiz wouldn't be content with sheep grazing but beyond that? Dad told me to keep on digging to try to discover the scumbag's agenda."

"Meaning?"

"We hacked his computer. I'm finalizing an awesome story. Contrasting the *colonias* and *maquiladora* workers' living conditions to the lavish game reserve. The consortium includes top execs of parent conglomerates and friends of Ortiz who want a little playground close to the Border. I can't write all this from here."

"Meaning?"

"I've been Zooming Mom, you'll be happy to hear. I'm flying to Singapore to write the story and produce a TV slot with her. She has the lowdown on some of the exotic animal smugglers in Southeast Asia and we're aiming to expose them. Expose that shit Ortiz. Once our story airs, it'll go viral."

"Flying to Singapore? When?"

"In a few days. Teresita's going with me to work on the story. Don't worry. Dad gave me all his frequent flyer miles. We could circle the globe several times first class! I owe Teresita big time," he said, reaching for her hands.

"Rory, slow down. Have you squared things with your professors? Is Penny organizing an internship they'll accept for your course work?"

"An *internship? Jeeez!* You just don't get it, do you? Who the hell needs a degree with a media break like this?" He glanced at his watch. "Crap. We need to go," he said to Teresita.

"That's it? You're just going to jump the country? When did you intend telling me? God, Rory, what about your *passport?*" I remembered it was still sealed in the APD crime lab.

"Passport?" He laughed. "Don't you remember Grandma helped me swing an Irish passport that time in high school I visited Cuba? "

Stunned, I turned to Teresita. "Does Isabel know?"

"We're on our way to tell her now," she said. "Like you, she won't be too happy."

"Hey, Buzz, thanks for everything," Rory butt in, scraping back his chair. "You're the best. Get a life, OK? Mom says visit us in Singapore. She has plenty of room."

After a hasty good-bye to them both, I sat like a statue, unwilling to allow myself a show of emotion as they paid, and walked out of the *Emporium.* Teresita was the only one to pause, look back at me, press her hand to her heart and wave.

I left voicemails for both Zuniga and Colleen to say I was on my way home.

Then I called Carlos and told him I'd be there later in the afternoon. To restore some sense of balance, I said, I sure hoped our whiteboard was overloaded with tasks, meetings and site visits I had to handle immediately.

*

So Penny, my dear former sister-in-law, there you have it, exactly as it happened within that sleepless week. You have the right to know all of this to fill in recent and past gaps in our family story. Impossible to give you every detail in Zooms and emails. I also needed to write it out of my system. Rory and Teresita are still with you now and that's a relief for me. One of the campus libraries is archiving Hugh's papers and collections from the storage area, which is exactly what he wanted. I was finally able to claim Al's head and a few scraps from the killing field. Sister Colleen, Joaquin and I buried what was left of Al wrapped in one of Hugh's shirts in a churchyard close to the Border. We lined the tiny plot with rose petals, and herbs from my garden. I planted milkweed on the grave to attract Monarch Butterflies.

The stone reads, in loving memory of Al Two Spirit de la Rosa McBride.

The perps were never found.

Afterword

My love of Austin, the Hill Country and West Texas prompted much of this story and I make no apologies for weaving a family tale around the horrors of conditions at the *maquiladoras* combined with the daily realities of lives dominated by the cartels and folks desperate for asylum. Snuff flicks have been associated in the past with the disappearances and dismemberment of young maquiladora workers in Juarez.

Re Austin—when I started crafting this book, the area around the Amtrak station downtown promised the funky little community of studios and renovated rail depots I describe. Some of the endearing character remains, but surrounded by tall skyscrapers in the rapid revitalization of downtown. I still love to walk and photograph that area, though I have taken many liberties with the site in this story.

Lady Bird Lake has all the shifting seasons, glorious trees, birds and butterflies honored here, enjoyed by scores of fellow cyclists, joggers and dog walkers.

Re West Texas—there is no Rio de la Luna, but the beauty I describe matches Rio Diablo which feeds the Rio Grande. I encourage all those interested in the unique rock art of the Lower Pecos River to visit www.SHUMLA.org to learn more about ongoing archeological research projects as well as the SHUMLA school in Comstock.

Private game reserves can—alas—be found in Texas, as reported in graphic detail by CBS *Sixty Minutes* on June 9, 2012. More information can also be tracked on the Humane Society and PETA websites.

Maquiladora working conditions continue to be disgraceful. Part of the proceeds of this book will be donated to *Austin Tan Cerca de la Frontera* for their ongoing support on behalf of those workers and their families.

Acknowledgments

My heartfelt thanks go to the following family members, friends and colleagues, for offering advice, checking facts, and for reading raw drafts of the work as it evolved over several years.

My incredible spouse Bernadette Winiker and my soulsisters Sophie Keir and Nancy Clancy, as well as my niece Dyan Ferguson and my middle brother Neil, read through various drafts and offered excellent suggestions. My youngest brother Jimmy, offered superb guidance as an architect.

Judy Blocklinger of Del Rio, Texas, shared her insights as a former P.I. turned acupuncturist. Judy also happens to have long family ties with the Border Patrol and a rugged sense of what it means to grow up on the Border.

Tess Sherman, (now retired) senior crime analyst and sketch artist, Austin Police Department, shared her many talented insights, guidance and friendship.

Shelia Hargis, crime analysis supervisor, Austin Police Department, shared her expertise generously.

Stacy Kazmir, forensic consultant, formerly of the Austin Police Department Forensic Science Division, gave her meticulous advice, even if I wove creative liberties around it!

Elvia Mendoza, PhD (anthropology), shared her insightful knowledge and research on gender violence.

John King, Austin-based attorney and former law professor, shared such witty advice!.

Rob Johnson, Austin-based attorney, shared his expertise on land inheritance tussles dating from historic Spanish Texas to modern Texas.

Elton Prewitt of the SHUMLA Foundation, archaeologist and expert in the cave rock art of the lower Pecos River area of West Texas was an invaluable guide. Elton's spirited tours provided remarkable insights when he took us to sites off the beaten track.

Tomas and Teri Rodriguez, retired bilingual teachers and my dear neighbors, have always been a wonderful resource, not only for Spanish colloquialisms, but for their willingness to read an early draft of the book.

Austin-based artist Shirley Ann Riley, a member of our Artemis group of women veterans, crafted the beautiful image on the front cover after our endless quest to hit just the right message.

Great buddy Suzanne Rittenberry's bilingual skills and crisp knowledge of Austin was so helpful. She campaigned together with the late Judy Rosenberg of *Austin'Tan Cerca de la Frontera,* and dear friends Josefina Castillo and Janet Cook, to alert all of us to the appalling labor situation in Border sweatshops *(maquiladoras)* and living conditions in the *colonias.*

Also my dear buddies Tina Huckabee of Austin, Angela Neustatter of London, Lizbeth Rice Johnson of Hawaii, and John Whalen of Austin all added their expert eyes and advice. Elaine Hampton, retired professor of U.T. El Paso and author, shared her phenomenal experience of the Border. Isaac Short, Austin- based architect, was a great tech sounding board.

My wonderful agents—Edy Selman (New York), David Grossman (London), Ruth Weibel and Suzanne De Roche (Zurich) have given endless support for decades.

Likewise my splendid editor friend and soulbrother Trent Duffy scoured and shaped the manuscript skillfully. Phil Whitmarsh, *Redbrush* co-founder and chief navigator, has been an inspiration through some fifteen years, and added the final deft touch to this book, along with graphic artist Ryan Simanek.

Norma Andrade, of *Bring our Daughters Home,* helped inspire

Crossing Lines when she campaigned in the United States on behalf of her daughter, Lilia, and over four hundred young women whose brutal murders in the killings fields of the Border town of Ciudad Juarez, Chihuahua Mexico, have yet to be fully investigated and resolved. Anthropoligst and author Cecilia Balli researched horrifying details she allowed me to share. And a word of honor for the late Diana Hamilton Russell whose tireless research on global femicide added another dimension to the Juarez killing fields.

My late father, Louis Wright Ferguson, a global geologist who trained at U.T. Austin, and grew up in El Paso, fascinated me with his endless Border stories And finally I honor my late mother, Pan Coombe Ferguson Robertson, who gave birth to me in the mine hospital of San Francisco del Oro, in the heart of Chihuahua Mexico, a few months after surviving a nightmare of an ocean journey from Africa to the USA, with Dad and my brothers, during WW2.

- PEF Austin 2020

About the Author

Pamela Ellen Ferguson calls Austin home after living and working as a journalist and award winning teacher of Asian Bodywork Therapy in over a dozen capitals across Europe, the Middle East, Southern Africa, Canada and the USA. She was born in Chihuahua Mexico and has authored ten books of fiction and non-fiction ranging from politics to architecture to children's literature. She holds dual American and British citizenship. Her website is www.pamelaferguson.net.

About the Front Cover Artist

Shirley Ann Riley is a multi-media artist, sculptor, mural and mosaic designer who has exhibited frequently in Austin as part of the **Artemis** women veterans art group, and in Black History month exhibits at the S.W. Seminary of the West, at the George Washington Carver Museum, and multiple times at the Sharon and Brian Moore Alternative Space Gallery, of the Unitarian Universalist church.